When his eyes opened that morning, Longarm saw Melissa bent over him, her naked breasts inches from his face.

"I came to you," she whispered. "I wanted to thank you."

"Thank me? You don't need to thank me, Melissa."

"But . . . I want to."

She leaned still closer, her incandescent breasts almost smothering him. Then, for what seemed like a delicious eternity, she took his lips with hers. But even as he felt his manhood responding, Longarm couldn't help but wonder if Melissa really could have been innocent in all that dirty business with the missing Mormon land trusts.

TABOR EVANS

LONGARM

AND THE
BLOODY TRACKDOWN

JOVE BOOKS, NEW YORK

LONGARM AND THE BLOODY TRACKDOWN

A Jove Book/published by arrangement with
the author

PRINTING HISTORY
Jove edition/January 1988

ISBN: 0-515-09378-5

Jove Books are published by The Berkley Publishing Group,
200 Madison Avenue, New York, New York 10016.
The name "JOVE" and the "J" logo
are trademarks belonging to Jove Publications, Inc.

PRINTED IN THE UNITED STATES OF AMERICA

10 9 8 7 6 5 4 3 2 1

Chapter One

Longarm flicked the remains of his coffee into the fire and stood up. An uncommonly tall, broad-shouldered man with an upswept longhorn mustache, his size made him loom somewhat ominously in the darkness.

"I don't believe you men," Longarm told the foreman and the rest of the cowpunchers standing around the fire. "I think Milt is out here—and if he ain't, you men sure as hell know where he is."

The foreman left the shadow of the chuckwagon and stepped closer. His name was Tim Prewitt. "Who are you, mister?" he asked Longarm belligerently. "And what do you want this feller for?"

"You're askin' if I'm a lawman?"

"That's what I'm askin'."

Longarm caught the foreman's smoldering gaze.

The fellow was built blockily, with a square, pugnacious face and an unruly shock of light hair that hung down over his forehead. He looked to be as tough as he sounded, and was at the moment determined to keep Milt out of the hands of what he perceived as a lawman bent on hauling him off—which meant Prewitt and the rest of this crew liked Milt and were willing to go out on a limb for him, even if that meant standing up to a lawman.

Longarm shrugged. His showing up like this made it impossible for Milt to keep undercover any longer. The moment Longarm rode into this cow camp, that part of the operation ended.

"All right, Prewitt," Longarm replied. "Suppose I am a lawman?"

Prewitt spat a heavy glob of chewing tobacco to the ground at Longarm's feet. "In that case we ain't tellin' you nothin'."

Someone piped up, "Hell! We ain't never heard of Milt Grumman."

Longarm grinned recklessly at the cowpoke. "Looks like you already told me what I needed to know. Milt's here, ain't he—and if he ain't, you know where he is."

"Damn you," snarled Prewitt. "There ain't no law says we have to let you take Milt. Get on your horse and clear out."

Longarm took a deep, patient breath. "Look. I rode out here for Milt because he's one of our men working out of the federal marshal's office in Denver. We ain't heard from him in too damn long. He signed up with this spread in Buffalo City. Now,

2

unless you men got something to hide, I suggest you tell me where in hell he is."

The foreman shifted uncomfortably and looked quickly around him at the cowpokes crowding around. With surprised mutters, they pulled back warily, some of them doing nothing to hide their anger.

"Shit," Prewitt said, "you mean you and Milt are lawmen?"

"You want to see my badge?"

Prewitt shook his head grimly, as much in wonder as in anger. "Goddamn! That sonofabitch sure had us fooled."

"Where is he?"

"In that wagon over there. He's been banged up pretty bad. You ain't heard from him because he got caught in a stampede. But before I take you over there, you mind telling me what fool reason a federal marshal would have for signing on with this outfit as a cowpoke?"

"He was lookin' for someone."

"And who might that be?"

"Someone who might be working for J. T. Roebuck."

"Hell, all of us here work for him."

"Well now, is any one of you Clint Bolen?"

"Marshal," Prewitt drawled, "we ain't never heard that name before. And you can flash all the badges you want at us, we won't none of us tell you any different."

"Then take me to Milt."

Prewitt led Longarm away from the campfire and across the dark ground to a wagon sitting under a big

3

cottonwood. Leaning into it, he called, "Hey, Milt. You got a visitor."

Longarm poked his head in. Milt was lying on his back, a blanket over him, a pillow under his head. He needed a haircut and a shave and, from the smell of him, a bath. Longarm looked back at Prewitt.

"Thanks, Prewitt."

As the foreman turned to go, he said, "I expect you and Milt to be gone soon as you can. We don't need no undercover marshals working on this spread."

"I'll keep that in mind,"

"Jesus, Longarm," said Milt, as Longarm stepped into the wagon. "Did you tell him who I was?"

"No way I could prevent it, Milt. How you feelin'?"

"My leg, Longarm. It's torn up bad. I need more help than I can get from Prewitt and his hands. I guess I'm pretty damn glad you showed up."

Longarm examined Milt's leg. It didn't take him long to realize Milt needed more help than Longarm could provide and that moving Milt from this wagon in his present condition would be disastrous.

"Christ, Milt," Longarm said, leaning back after his examination. "How long you been like this?"

"The stampede was two weeks ago, a couple of hundred miles from here. I been in this wagon ever since. We only just reached Roebuck's spread."

"You got a line on Bolen?"

"Not yet. But I been hearin' things."

"Like what?"

"That he's already in Ridge City and has a deal cookin' with J. T. Roebuck."

4

"Anything more?"

"Sorry, Longarm. I just ain't been in any condition to nose around. He was with the outfit when I joined it in Buffalo City, and I expected to run into him on the trail drive north. But he never showed. Seems he took the easy way north—the train."

"Was Melissa Barstow with him?"

"There was talk he was with a girl. That's why he took the train. But I never saw her."

"I'm going into town to get a doc for that leg of yours. Maybe I'll find Bolen and the girl. I might even be able to talk them into going back to Salt Lake City."

"Good luck," Milt said wearily, lying his head back down on the pillow.

Longarm stepped down from the wagon and glanced over at the chuckwagon. Prewitt and his punchers were still standing around the campfire, watching him. Longarm was going to have to leave Milt in their care. He didn't much like the idea, since Prewitt and the rest of his men would no longer feel anything for Milt but resentment. By living and working among them as someone other than who he was, he had tricked and deceived them. No one liked an impostor, no matter how noble or necessary the reason for the deception.

As Longarm walked back to the chuckwagon, Prewitt came to meet him.

"I'm going into Ridge City for a doctor," Longarm told the foreman. "Is there one in town?"

"Sure. Doc Farnsworth."

"Where can I find him?"

5

"He's a lush, but a good enough doctor. He hangs out in the Lucky Lady."

"I won't be long."

"You think Milt's leg is that bad?"

"I just want a doctor to look at it before we move him."

"Go ahead. We'll keep an eye on him—even if he is a lawman."

"That's right decent of you," Longarm said, heading for his horse. He was in no mood for further discussion. He was in a hurry.

As Longarm rode through the black, moonless night, he shook his head ruefully. It was always the way, he commented to himself. The simplest assignments always turned into the most nettlesome. A lapsed Mormon gal takes off with her boyfriend and it turns into something a hell of a lot more complicated when they find out she's taken valuable Mormon records with her.

For the Mormons, genealogical records were vital, what with all them wives and their gangs of offspring to keep track of; for only with accurate records could the church be certain who was married to whom, who fathered whom—and more important, which Mormon owned what. The Mormon genealogical records taken by Melissa Barstow dealt with the descendants of an early settlement in Idaho, including the deeds they drew up, the land transfers they made—in short, who had legal title to the farms, ranches, and grazing land in the area.

What Melissa—or her lover Clint Bolen— wanted with those Mormon chronicles Longarm had no idea. Neither had Marshal Billy Vail. And they would not find out until they overtook Bolen and the girl. The bigwigs in Salt Lake City weren't talking, either. They were petrified with fear that news of this theft would leak out, panicking those devout Mormons who relied on the chronicles' accuracy to guarantee them and their ancestors an unimpeded passage to the pearly gates.

On the face of it, tracing the two decamped lovers had seemed a simple enough assignment. But it had proven anything but easy after the two vanished completely from sight after leaving Salt Lake City. A month ago Billy Vail got word that Bolen had been in Buffalo City, Kansas, purchasing cattle for J. T. Roebuck and his Land and Cattle Company, an outfit that owned half of Montana and most of Idaho. That was when Longarm suggested to Billy Vail an acquaintance of his who was anxious to try his spurs as a U.S. federal marshal. A working cowpoke until recently, Milt Grumman easily passed muster with Vail and was sent to join the cattle purchased by J. T. Roebuck on their drive up from Kansas, in hopes Milt might be able to collar Bolen in the process.

But all Milt had managed to do was break a leg trying to turn a stampede.

Longarm liked Milt Grumman, and he was worried a lot more than he had let on to him about that broken leg. He had never seen one that looked—or smelled—that bad. At that moment, as Longarm rode on through the black night toward Ridge City, it was Milt Grumman's leg that worried him, not Clint Bolen and Melissa Barstow, nor those Mormon chronicles she had run off with; the way it looked to

7

Longarm, if he didn't get a doctor out to him fast, there was a chance Milt would lose his right leg.

Longarm glanced up at the sky. No stars, no moon. It felt like he was riding through a sewer pipe with no light at the end of it. He became aware of a massive bluff looming out of the night ahead of him. He slowed his mount to move out around it. The pound of hoofs coming up fast behind him suddenly filled the night. Before he could turn to see who it was, a rope snaked out of the darkness and settled over his shoulders, pinning both arms. An instant later he felt himself dragged backward, his feet lifting from his stirrups. He began to turn slowly in mid-air, and knew he should brace himself for the coming impact. But he had no time as he slammed brutally onto the hard-packed ground and tumbled into a darkness more profound than the one he had been galloping through. . . .

It was raining. The heavy drops were pounding down on his face with a relentless persistence. Longarm tried to open his eyes, but he lids were heavy, ponderously heavy, like his arms and legs and all the rest of him. He could not move. Only through enormous effort was he able to open his eyes, the lids lifting just enough to allow him a glimpse of the two horsemen looming over him in the wet night.

Bent under the downpour's relentless hammering, the two men sat on their horses and peered down at Longarm, the rain pouring off their hat brims in steady rivulets. It was their voices that had aroused him—that as much as the pounding rain. They were discussing him calmly enough. How to dispose of

8

him. Their voices were barely audible. And Longarm could not make out their faces.

". . . you want him on your tail the rest of your life?" the smaller of the two demanded.

"No, dammit," his companion replied uneasily. "But this is murder."

The reply was a harsh oath. "We're gettin' wet sittin' here. You want me to finish him off for you?"

"No, dammit. I'll do it."

The larger of the two nudged his horse closer and Longarm caught the wet shine of gunmetal in the rider's hand. As he loomed closer, Longarm tried desperately to reach back with his right hand to palm the weapon resting in his vest's watch-fob pocket— a derringer attached to his watch by a gold chain. But he still could not move a muscle. He was caught in one of those nightmares he used to have, where his feet were embedded in cement and a runaway stage was bearing down on him. The figure on the horse aimed his weapon carefully through the driving rain.

Go ahead, you bastard, Longarm thought. *Go ahead. But do it clean, you sonofabitch!*

The sixgun detonated. A flame from its muzzle lanced through the rain. The bullet struck Longarm on the side of his forehead and glanced off without entering his skull. At that distance, however, the bullet hit with the impact of a crowbar, slamming Longarm's head around and snapping his nose as it drove his face into the ground.

With his head still ringing, Longarm felt a hand clamp down upon his right shoulder and fling him roughly onto his back again. He felt the blood pouring from his nostrils, filling his half-open mouth.

9

"He's finished," Longarm heard dimly.

He could not open his eyes. Both eye sockets were filled solidly with mud, the pelting rain driving it deeper into the corners of his eyes. The rope that was still about his chest was tugged suddenly tighter. He heard hoofbeats start up and then felt himself being dragged along the mud-slick ground. A moment later the horse lifted to a gallop.

Longarm felt himself crashing through brush and slamming over boulders slick with rain. The pounding was interminable, and he felt himself losing consciousness. At last the horse swerved and Longarm felt the ground fall away from under him as the rider swung him out over the lip of a steep arroyo, then cut him loose.

For a moment Longarm floated painlessly through space. Then his left shoulder struck a soft ledge and he began to cartwheel helplessly, crunching through mesquite until he slammed facedown into the muddy stream that surged through the wash. The force of the current was enough to catch him up at once and pull him swiftly along until it drove him hard up onto a sandbank, pushing his head and shoulders out of the water.

Clinging to a bush, Longarm heard the distant murmur of voices above the roar of the water and at once let the heavy liquid pluck him from the bank and carry him farther along until he struck against the side of a large boulder. He kept himself close under it for a moment, then allowed himself to be pulled on past it and around a sharp bend into suddenly deep, turbulent water. As he twisted slowly in the rushing

10

water, he heard the dim mutter of pounding hoofs fading in the distance.

He swam on through the dark, silted water and clambered at last onto a rocky shore and collapsed facedown upon the ground. Completely and utterly exhausted, he found nevertheless that the terrible immobility that had turned his limbs to lead was gone. But he could no longer keep his eyes open. The feel of the pounding rain faded as he drifted off into oblivion.

When he awoke it was daylight—a cheerless gray light that barely lit the ground around him. The infernal rain was still coming down. His teeth were chattering from the clammy chill of his sodden clothing; and in fact there was not a square inch of his entire body that was not protesting the pounding he had received.

He pushed himself up off the ground and felt the furrow the slug had plowed in the side of his forehead. First the muddy water and now the rain was keeping it clean. It was not all that deep, he realized —and soon enough his hair would grow back to cover it. He was lucky. Luckier than he deserved to be, he noted grimly as he turned himself around and sat with his back against a rock and tried to take stock. Who those two men were, and why they wanted to kill him, he had no idea. But one phrase keep going over and over in Longarm's head.

"... *you want him on your tail the rest of your life?*"

And that query seemed to point to Clint Bolen. But why the hell should Bolen think Longarm would stay on his trail for the rest of his life just because he ran off with a horny dame? Eloping was not a hanging offense, not even if the girl *was* a Mormon. And those damn Mormon chronicles the girl had taken with her could hardly be all that important—no matter how unhappy their theft made those Mormon officials in Salt Lake City.

At the moment, however, one thing only was certain. Whoever those two men were, Longarm would find them. Their voices, if not their faces, would remain forever implanted in his memory, and he would not need a warrant from Billy Vail to go after them, either.

But time enough for that later. Milt still needed a doctor for that rotting leg of his. Slowly, painfully, Longarm got to his feet. Muscles he had never heard from before in his life protested the action. Gingerly, Longarm tested the bones and found nothing broken. But all the hinges and bolts had sure as hell been loosened some—and nothing, it seemed, could make the pounding in his head simmer down.

Squinting up through the rain, Longarm spied a path he could take out of the wash. Loosening the rope that was still snugged about his chest, he lifted it over his head, coiled it, then started up the embankment toward the rim. It was a long climb. The wet clay and gravel made it no easier, but he reached solid ground without incident, stood up, and peered through the steady downpour in hopes of catching sight of his horse. But all he saw was the shifting curtain of rain that enclosed him on all sides.

He started to walk, his eyes peering intently

through the rain at the ground. He lost track of the distance he traveled, aware only that he should be getting closer to the spot where he was flung from his horse. He stopped. His horse was standing as silent and immobile as a statue in the driving rain less than twenty yards from him. Its head was down, its long tail soaked and heavy and hanging straight to the ground. And in the mud just in front of the horse, his hat was resting on its brim.

Reaching the hat, Longarm plucked it out of the mud, wiped the sweatband as clean as he could, then fitted it gingerly down upon his aching head and the long, still tender gash in his scalp. Next he moved closer to the dun, calling softly to it. The animal's ears went flat and its nostrils flared as it watched Longarm approach through the shifting curtains of rain. Longarm called out a second time. This seemed to reassure the horse. Still, it watched him warily, its ears still flat.

Still speaking to it softly, Longarm took hold of the hanging reins and pulled the horse closer. Until that moment Longarm had not realized just how sore he was. Carefully fitting his boot into the stirrup, he pulled himself into the saddle and hauled his right leg over the cantle. As he straightened in the saddle, the universe swung drunkenly around his head for a moment. Longarm waited for it to settle back into its usual orbit, then hauled the dun around.

He felt a lot better now with a solid mount under him, and as he rode, he checked the double-action .44 resting in his cross-draw rig. It was serviceable, he figured, but he would have to clean it thoroughly as soon as he reached Ridge City. His derringer sat snugly in his vest pocket, and his Winchester still rested in his saddle scabbard. But so he didn't get to thinking it was going to be all sunshine and roses from here on, the rain began to pound down all the heavier.

Reaching back behind the cantle for his slicker, he pulled it on, then bent his body into the slanting rain and continued on through the roaring darkness.

Chapter Two

It was close to the dawn of another day when Longarm picked out the trail that tilted into the long valley
opening ahead of him. He could just make out the
tracks bisecting the valley and, on the far side of it,
the disorderly cluster of buildings comprising Ridge
City. Because there was as yet no direct rail link from
the Union Pacific to the newly constructed Idaho
Southern line, Longarm had chosen to ride across
country, passing through the sprawling ranch lands
belonging to the Roebuck Land and Cattle Company
headquartered here in Ridge City.

The rain was letting up only slightly as Longarm
clopped over a wooden bridge which spanned a
swollen, raging torrent, then turned left onto a dim,
unlighted main street now fetlock-deep in mud.
Through the shifting curtains of rain, he noted the

many new false-front clapboard buildings, most of them still unpainted. The size of the unfinished train depot and the new hotel looming ahead of him indicated that since the arrival of the Idaho Southern Railroad, Ridge City was prospering.

Longarm swung his horse out of the rain into the livery stable across the hotel. Dismounting, he found the hostler asleep on a blanket inside the grain room. He shook the old man awake and told him to grain the dun, then took a long, grateful stretch. His need for sleep was a strong tide threatening to pull him under.

"Doc Farnsworth's the only sawbones in town, I understand," Longarm said to the hostler.

"Nope," the old man said, leading the dun into a stall. "But he's the best of a bad lot. The rest're just snake-oil salesmen and bleeders."

Longarm hefted his gear onto his shoulder and, lugging his Winchester in his right hand, left the stable and moved through the rain to the hotel across the street. He wanted to wash the mud and grime off himself before he slept, but he wondered if he would be able to postpone sleep for that long.

As it turned out, he couldn't. The moment he opened the door to his room and saw the bed, he stumbled over to it. He flung his gear down and, despite his nagging concern for Milt, was asleep seconds after he kicked off his sopping wet boots.

It was late that same afternoon and still raining when Longarm emerged from the hotel. He had taken a steaming hot bath in a back room of the hotel for twenty-five cents, and the hotel tailor had done what he could to clean up and repair his soaked duds. Now, hungry and parched, he was eager to fill his belly and find that doctor for Milt.

Leaning into the cold, wind-driven rain, he moved along the board walk until he found a small restaurant, where he feasted on steak and fries, topped off with a thick wedge of apple pie, and washed down with three steaming mugs of black coffee. Then he paid up and left, heading on down the boardwalk to the Lucky Lady in hopes of locating the doctor for Milt.

Shouldering through the batwings, he found himself in a surprisingly spacious saloon, one considerably more opulent than he would have expected in an Idaho town this isolated. Again, he attributed this to the prosperity brought in by the railroad. A long mirror ran the length of the bar, and the walls were filled with oversized paintings of lusty females rendered with great enthusiasm and a good deal of healthy exaggeration. Longarm glanced casually at them as he bellied up to the highly polished mahogany bar. Ordering a beer, he looked around.

The saloon was long, with a ceiling at least twenty feet high, and was almost as wide as it was deep. A broad staircase led up to a balcony, off which many doors opened—the bar girls' cribs, Longarm realized. Even at this early hour, a steady stream of customers moved up the stairs with the girls in tow. Longarm paid for his beer and picked his way through the thick coils of smoke to a table along the back wall, near the poker and faro tables. Here the stench of wet, unwashed feet seemed less overpowering.

Sitting with his hatbrim slanted down over his forehead, Longarm kept his eyes and ears open. It was not only the doctor he hoped to find. If Milt was right and Clint Bolen was already here, there was a good chance he might show up in this saloon—if, that was, he could tear himself away from his lady love. Leaning back in his chair, Longarm sipped his beer, becoming aware as he did so of the quiet, authoritative voice of the faro dealer close by to his left.

When he heard the dealer refer to one of the players as "Doc," he came alert at once. Glancing at the player the dealer had addressed, Longarm saw the back of a man who was wearing a threadbare frock coat and a somewhat battered bowler hat tipped rakishly to one side. The fellow's stiff white collar was loose and not overly clean, and he obviously needed a haircut.

The faro dealer was laughing now at the doctor, who had evidently requested an extension of credit. The other faro players joined in the merriment, their harsh, barking laughter causing the doctor to shrug and back away from the table. He was about to head for the bar when Longarm called out to him softly.

"Doctor Farnsworth . . . ?"

The man stopped and looked over at Longarm, his bloodshot eyes going crafty, as if he were sighting down a long gun barrel at a sucker—that is, someone who might be foolish enough to advance him the wherewithal for a drink. Reaching for a filthy handkerchief he kept in his sleeve, he dabbed nervously, hopefully, at his mouth and managed a smile.

"At your service, sir," he said, pulling to a stop by

18

Longarm's table. "But I am afraid you have the advantage of me."

"Name's Long. Custis Long. I was hoping you might join me in a drink, Doctor."

"Well, now," the doc said, "I don't usually accept libations from strangers—but I suppose I could make an exception in your case, sir. No sense in letting one's principles stand in the way of one's weaknesses."

"Then by all means join me."

The doctor slumped wearily down in a chair beside Longarm. Longarm waved over a bar girl, then glanced at the doctor, who ordered a double shot of whiskey and a beer chaser. Then, rubbing his mouth in anticipation, he turned his full attention on Longarm.

"Is this business, my friend? A sportive spleen, perhaps? An ache in the bones?"

Longarm shook his head.

"Well, then. Thank you. But I must warn you. My office hours have come—and gone."

He smiled in grateful anticipation as his drinks were placed in front of him. Longarm paid the girl and studied the doctor. He was a physical wreck, a scrawny ghost of a man, and on his hollow cheeks Longarm saw the hectic flush of the consumptive.

Farnsworth caught the pity in Longarm's eyes. Finishing his whiskey, he threw the beer down after it, then wiped his mouth. "I note you are cognizant of my frail condition, Mr. Long."

Longarm shrugged.

"It is true. I am near death," the doctor admitted grandly, as if he were an actor relishing his role. "In-

19

deed, every time I look in a mirror, I see, not myself, but Death, peering out at me through these hollow sockets. You have noted, I can see, the flush on my cheeks, that cruel counterfeit of health put there by a sportive fate."

"'Physician, heal thyself.'"

"Ah, but there's the rub. There is no physician for me but God—or Satan."

"A friend of mine needs your help, Doc," Longarm said quietly, "and if we don't hurry, maybe *his* next physician will be God."

"And where might this friend of yours be?"

Longarm waved at the bar girl to bring the doctor another round. "He's some distance from here, on the J. T. Roebuck spread. He's got a broken leg that needs mending."

"My dear sir, it is raining."

"The leg is in bad shape, Doc. He needs you."

"I do not make house calls. Nor do I make calls on farflung ranges, and surely not in such inclement weather."

Farnsworth's second round arrived. As Longarm paid, the doctor lifted the glass in grateful salute to him, then threw the fiery liquid down his hatch. As the doctor followed it with his beer chaser, Longarm glanced up and saw three men entering the saloon. From the description Longarm had memorized, the one following the others in could have been Clint Bolen. Who the other two were, he had no idea.

"Those three men just coming in," Longarm said, indicating them with a nod of his head. "Who are they?"

"Don't know all three. But the little gent with the

round face and gimlet eyes, the one with the cigar—
that's J. T. Roebuck himself, the owner of the Idaho
Southern Railroad and just about everything else in
these parts."

"And the one behind him?"

"Never seen him before. But that wiry little one in
front of J. T. is the gent you better watch out for."

"Why?"

"He's Tate Rawson. J. T.'s bodyguard. That's a
polite name for hired killer."

Longarm looked more closely at Tate Rawson.
There was something about the little man's shape that
reminded him of someone. Longarm would like to
see how he sat a horse in the rain. He would be sure
then. His clean-shaven face was thin and predatory,
and his eyes, as they glanced quickly about him,
were cold and deadly, like holes in a corpse.

As the three continued on through the saloon,
J. T. Roebuck waved over one of the bar girls, then
took her with him as he and his two companions
threaded their way past friendly patrons, then moved
on up the stairs. A moment later they had disappeared into one of the rooms off the balcony. As the
three men had moved toward the staircase, Longarm
had been careful to keep his hat brim pulled well
down over his face. He was not absolutely certain,
but there was a likelihood that two of those three men
he just watched file by him had sat their horses in a
downpour the night before and calmly decided to kill
him.

But for now, they would just have to wait.

Longarm glanced back at the doctor. Farnsworth
had been drinking pretty steadily since dropping into

the chair at Longarm's table. Yet he appeared more competent now than he had then. Taking off his hat, Longarm placed it down on the table and with the same motion drew his derringer. Thumbcocking it, he thrust it under the hat, allowing the tip of its muzzle to poke out from under the brim—straight at the doc's chest. Startled, the doctor glanced quickly about for help. But Longarm's move had been too quick for anyone to have noticed.

"I want you to come with me now, Doc," Longarm told the man.

"I told you. I do not make house calls."

"This time you will," Longarm told him, his voice gaining an edge sharp enough to cut through the doctor's alcoholic haze.

Blinking, the doc peered closer at Longarm, frowning as he studied the slash on the side of Longarm's head and then the swollen nose. "First of all," he said, "we're going to my office so I may pack that broken nose of yours, and then see to that mean gash in your scalp. After which I shall have another drink. I'll need it if I'm going anywhere in this miserable weather."

Longarm slipped his derringer back into his vest pocket and put his hat back on. "All right, Doc," he said, getting to his feet. "It's a deal. But you go first."

Weaving slightly, the doctor preceded Longarm out of the saloon.

The rain had let up some by the time they approached the wagon where Longarm had left Milt Grumman the night before. The wagon still sat under the cottonwood, but the chuckwagon was gone, and there was no sign of Prewitt or any of his cowpokes. Riding through the flat, undulating country, Longarm had already noted that the large herd had moved on.

Now, as he dismounted and walked swiftly up to the wagon, he felt an icy premonition of disaster. Only when he glanced into the wagon and saw Milt's sleeping form did he relax.

He turned to the doctor, who was slogging through the mud after him. "In here, Doc," Longarm told him. "He's asleep, looks like."

With a weary sigh, Farnsworth pulled himself up into the wagon, put his black bag beside Milt, and shook his shoulder to waken him. He shook it again, peered closer at the man, then leaned wearily back.

"What is it?" Longarm asked.

"Your friend does not need to have his broken leg reset."

"What do you mean?"

"There's a bullet in his skull—or, more accurately, a bullet has passed clean through it. Your friend is dead. Has been, I would say, for more than twenty-four hours."

Longarm stepped up into the wagon and crouched beside Farnsworth. Milt was dead, all right, his eyes staring straight up and past him, cold and unblinking, like a kid's marbles. Jesus. Longarm felt sick. But why was he surprised? Two men had done their best to kill him. With Milt they had succeeded.

"Let's get back to Ridge City, Doc," Longarm said.

"I'm the coroner for this county," Farnsworth said. "I'll send the undertaker out. And J. T. Roe-

23

buck should be notified. This murder took place on his land."

"I'll notify him, Doc."

"Oh?"

"I'm a deputy U.S. marshal out of Denver. And this here was my partner."

Farnsworth was surprised. His eyebrows shot up a notch. "Well, now, Marshal. It occurs to me you should take better care of your partners."

Longarm looked coldly at the doctor. He wanted to hit the man, but realized it would do no good. Farnsworth had no idea how deep that barb had sunk. He was too tired and too filled with cheap whiskey.

And dammit, the sonofabitch was right. Maybe if he had got back here sooner, he would have saved Milt from this. Maybe. Anyway, he could sure as hell take the measure of those who had murdered him. It wouldn't look very good if he allowed Milt's murder to go unchallenged. A U.S. marshal could not go around letting his partners get knocked off like this. Vail would certainly understand that.

But it didn't make any difference if Billy Vail did or not. Longarm understood it, and that was good enough for him.

Clint Bolen entered Melissa's room, kissed her absently, then walked over to the window and pulled the curtains open wider so he could peer down at the rain-swept street. He couldn't believe all this rain. He shivered slightly. But it was not from the dampness outside; instead, it came from the awful chill within him. In his mind's eye he could see still that poor sonofabitch in the wagon when Tate put that bullet through his head—and then that other lawman Tate had goaded Clint into killing. If he had known the price he would have to pay for this spread of his, he wondered if he would ever have taken that first step—for once having taken it, the other steps down this dark path had been inevitable. There was no turning back now. Ever.

"What is it, Clint?"

Clint turned to Melissa. "Nothing. I was just watching all this damn rain come down."

"Is that all you're going to do? Watch the rain? My God, can't we go somewhere, Clint? I didn't come all this way just to be cooped up in a hotel room."

Melissa sounded petulant—and of course she was. She was other things as well: lovely, sweet, desirable. And spoiled rotten. As filled with the devil as he was himself.

"I'm sorry, Mel," he said. "I guess sitting up here all this time hasn't been much fun for you, has it?"

"No, it hasn't."

She was wearing the green tailored suit he had always admired. Its color went well with her cat-eyes and fiery hair. The milky paleness of her complexion was a sharp contrast to the violence of her hair and the fire that turned her eyes to flaming jewels at times.

"Well, just think of it this way, Mel," he said. "Most of those cattle I bought for Roebuck in Kansas will end up on our ranch. Fact is, I came up to tell you to get ready. I'm going over to J. T.'s office in a minute to close the deal. We're through with him now, Mel. We're on our way at last."

Melissa's eyes went wide. "We're leaving here?"

"Tonight. We're taking the train north to Pine Ridge."

She jumped up from the bed. "I can't believe it!"

"Believe it, Mel."

She flung herself into his arms. "And will you marry me there?"

"Of course!"

"But, Clint, why not marry me now, this afternoon? Before we go."

"Mel, there's no time for that."

She saw the sudden resolve in his eyes and decided not to press the matter. "All right, Clint. All right. Just so I get out of this hotel room and this wet, miserable town."

"After I see Roebuck, I'll get the train tickets. The next train's due out of here at six."

"I'll be ready. Don't you worry."

"That's my girl."

He left the room and hurried out of the hotel and across the street to the Lucky Lady. On the second-floor balcony, he knocked on Roebuck's door and squared his shoulders nervously. He never liked dealing with Roebuck in his private office while his henchmen—Tate Rawson, especially—watched every move like wolves waiting to pounce.

Footsteps approached the door, heavy footsteps. That would mean the sheriff. The door was yanked open. Clint forced a smile.

"Hi, sheriff."

Tuttle turned his head. "It's Clint, J. T."

"Come in, Clint," Roebuck called.

Clint stepped inside. The sheriff pushed the door

shut, then waddled over to an easy chair and collapsed into it. J. T. was behind his desk, and Tate Rawson was asleep on the sofa. As Clint approached his desk, Roebuck looked past him at the sheriff. His glance was cold.

"Why don't you check downstairs, Tuttle?" Roebuck told him. "Make sure no one's breaking up the furniture. Clint and I got private business here."

"Sure thing, J. T.," Tuttle said quickly, heaving himself out of the easy chair and scrambling out the door.

As soon as it slammed shut behind him, Roebuck looked up at Clint. "All set, are you?"

"Melissa's packing now."

"And you want to take the six o'clock train this evening."

"I've done everything I said I would, Mr. Roebuck. You have the Mormon records you wanted. And the cattle are on their way north to your Circle R spread outside of Pine Ridge."

Roebuck smiled. "And our two meddling lawmen are dead."

Clint swallowed unhappily. "Yes."

Like a large, lazy serpent, Tate stirred, his cold, lidded eyes opening to focus on Clint. "Now you're one of us, Clint," he said. "Remember that. Last night you lost your cherry."

The terrible truth in Tate's words made Clint wince.

"Shut up, Tate," said Roebuck. "No need to go into that."

Looking back up at Clint, Roebuck smiled. But it was only the mouth that smiled. Roebuck's sharp, shoe-button eyes did not change expression at all as they regarded Clint coldly, calculatingly.

"You've had a chance to look at them chronicles, J. T.," Clint reminded him. "So I'd like that deed you promised me, the one to my ranch—and the bill of sale for them cattle. And the money."

"Of course, Clint. Of course. I have it all here, waiting for you."

Roebuck pulled open his drawer and lifted out a small steel strongbox and placed it down on top of his desk. Unlocking it with one of the keys on his gold keychain, he took from it the deed and the bill of sale Clint had asked for and handed them up to him.

As Clint placed the deed and the bill of sale in his billfold, Roebuck counted out the two thousand dollars he had agreed to pay Clint and Melissa for their delivery to him of the Mormon chronicles. Watching Roebuck count out the money reminded Clint how pleased Roebuck was that there would now be no way for any of the Mormon settlers to dispute his title to the most valuable land anywhere in Idaho, including the right-of-way for his Idaho Southern Railroad. Roebuck was counting heavily on linking his railroad later with the Great Northern line.

Finished counting out the money, Roebuck glanced up at Clint. "There you go, Clint," he said, pushing the bank notes across the desk to him. "It's a pleasure doing business with you."

"Thank you, J. T."

"It was a pleasure for me, too," said Tate Rawson, sitting up on the sofa and grinning at Clint. "You learn fast, mister. If you'd hang around I could show you and that filly of yours a few more tricks."

"No, thanks, Tate," Clint said, his mouth suddenly dry.

"Give my regards to the future little woman," said Roebuck, getting to his feet and extending his hand.

Clint shook it, heard himself mumble something appropriate, and then fled from the office, his head reeling slightly as it dawned on him what he had achieved—and what he had had to do in order to accomplish it. As he left the saloon a moment later, however, his head cleared abruptly and he became acutely aware of the bulging wallet in his inside pocket—and of the lovely and very grateful Melissa waiting for him in their hotel room, all packed and ready to go.

He put his head down and slogged through the mud toward the depot to get their tickets, aware that he still had more than two hours before the train pulled in. He wondered if that would be enough time to bed Melissa. He grinned suddenly. Knowing Melissa, it would be plenty of time. He increased his pace.

Chapter Three

Longarm arrived back in Ridge City with Doctor Farnsworth well past the supper hour—weary, wet, and heartsick. As he left the livery with the doctor, he reached into one of the saddlebags draped over his shoulder and dug out two cartwheels.

Dropping them into the doctor's waiting palm, he asked, "Will this cover things, Doc?"

"It should be sufficient. Yes. I'm sorry—about your partner, I mean."

"I'm sorry too, Doc."

"Why not join me in a drink after I go see the undertaker? It might do you some good. Take the chill off, anyway."

"Not the chill I'm feeling, Doc. Thanks anyway."

"As you say, Mr. Long. Perhaps later."

"Yeah, later, Doc. You goin' over to the Lady?"

"I guess I might at that."

"Do me a favor."

"If it is within my province to grant, ask away."

"I need to know more about them three gents we saw going upstairs. I'd like to know the name of the third one, the fellow you said you never saw before. And I'd also like to know if he's still up there with Roebuck and Tate Rawson."

"You don't want much."

"I'd sure appreciate it, Doc."

"I shall do my best."

"And use discretion."

"Sir, I am the very soul of discretion."

The doctor left Longarm then, darting through the heavy traffic of wagons and saddle horses toward the undertaker's establishment next to the Lucky Lady. It was also, Longarm noted, a barber shop.

As soon as Farnsworth disappeared into the shop, Longarm set off for the telegraph office to wire Billy Vail.

Not expecting or desiring an immediate reply from Billy Vail, Longarm returned to his hotel room. After a short nap, he went back to the livery stable, taking all his gear with him. He saddled his horse carefully, then told the hostler to keep his mount just inside the wide stable door at the rear until he came for it.

"You understand that, old man? When I come back here fore this mount, I want it all ready. I just might be leaving in a hurry."

The hostler shrugged. He was fully aware that something was up—and smart enough not to ask questions.

32

"And see you keep your mouth shut," Longarm warned. "Let it flap and you'll just be another stove-up cowpoke stretched out in horseshit."

To take some of the sting out of his words, Longarm tossed him a silver dollar and left the stable, crossing the street through the steady rain as he headed for the Lucky Lady. Before he entered it, he squinted up through the rain at the white railing that had been built along the edge of the first floor's roof. The second floor was set back from the first floor about two feet, leaving a narrow passageway between it and the clapboards. A man could make his way along it unseen from the street below, providing he kept his ass down.

Shouldering his way into the saloon, Longarm picked out Farnsworth apparently enjoying a run of luck at one of the faro tables. He caught the doc's eye, then ordered a beer and took it over to a table in a corner.

The saloon was crowded. Thick, pungent clouds of cigar smoke hung low over the bar and gaming tables. The stench of unwashed feet and soiled garments soaked from the rain mingled with that of whiskey and spilled beer. Constant, shattering bursts of laughter from the men crowding the bar or leaning over the gaming tables threatened to drown out the indefatigable piano player, a small fellow in a blue pin-striped shirt with red sleeve-garters and a black fedora perched jauntily on the side of his head. Five couples hopped about in the narrow space between the bar and the gaming tables, their clumsy foot-stomping only a crude prelude to a somewhat more basic dance they would attend to later upstairs.

Leaning back, Longarm sipped his beer and considered matters as they now stood. His telegram to Marshal Billy Vail in Denver had been short and to the point. He had not yet recovered the stolen Mormon documents, but he was pretty certain that J. T. Roebuck was involved in the theft and might now have them. Melissa Barstow and Clint Bolen were still at large. Milt Grumman was dead and Longarm was tracking those he thought were the killers. He ended the telegram with the statement that he did not need or want expense money and that he might be out of contact for some time.

Vail would understand. Longarm was going after Milt Grumman's killer at his own expense. The U.S. marshal would know there was nothing he could do about it. He was trapped behind a desk in Denver. Events were out of his hands.

Doc Farnsworth loomed over Longarm's table. He looked pleasantly spiffled and somewhat prosperous, as well.

"Had some luck, did you?" Longarm inquired.

Farnsworth sat down. "Indeed I did." He winked. "And not only at the tables."

"I'm listening."

"The barkeep is a pleasant man, a gentleman of the old school. It also happens he knows where the bodies are buried."

"Get to it, will you, Doc?"

"Am I to present my information with a dry whistle? Have you no compassion for an old reprobate?"

"Old reprobate is right," Longarm said, grinning. He waved a bar girl over.

Farnsworth ordered his usual poison and when it

was brought, he downed it without deliberation, then leaned back in his chair smacking his lips. "The individual whose name and person I had no knowledge of is a young man known to J. T. Roebuck as Clint Bolen. He is traveling with a very beautiful lady friend."

"A redhead?"

Farnsworth nodded. "And a very beautiful one, at that."

"Go on."

"You wanted to know if he was still up there. Well, I am afraid he is not. He has left town, I understand—on the six o'clock train for Pine Ridge."

Longarm was disappointed. He had hoped to collar him the same time he retrieved the Mormon chronicles, since there was little doubt now who Melissa Barstow had stolen them for—and why.

"What about the other one? Tate Rawson."

"He's still upstairs in Roebuck's office, I believe. He usually sticks pretty close to his boss."

"Thanks, Doc. You've been a great help."

"A word of advice."

"I'm listening."

"If you are going to do any . . . chastising up there, you should know that the local sheriff—his name is Jim Tuttle—is owned, body and soul, by Roebuck. He's got a deputy on guard in front of Roebuck's door. You ain't goin' to be able to storm in there, I'm thinking."

"Thanks for the tip."

Farnsworth pushed himself erect. "And now I will try my luck once more at the gaming tables. Will you be here for the funeral of your partner?"

"If I'm not, will you take care of it for me?"

"Of course."

Longarm reached into his pocket for more money, but the doctor held his hand up to restrain him. "That will not be necessary, Mr. Long. I have already been sufficiently recompensed."

"Thanks, Doc."

As the doctor walked over to a faro table, Longarm left the table and pushed himself through the crush to the bar. As he bellied up to it and ordered another beer, he caught the eye of a small, dark-haired bar girl a bit too plump for her trade. She was obviously on the lookout for someone not too particular. Longarm raised his stein to her in salute and smiled. She returned the smile almost gratefully and started for him.

"You want to help me get rid of my troubles?" Longarm suggested, as soon as she was near enough to hear him above the din.

"That's why I'm here, Tex," she said. "My name is Sadie. What's yours?"

"You got it right enough the first time," Longarm told her.

He took a swallow of his beer and looked around, frowning at the crowd and the noise. "There sure as hell ain't much room down here."

"There sure ain't, at that," Sadie agreed, reaching back to fix her hair, batting her eyelashes in an effort to appear seductive.

"Where's your crib?" he asked. "Upstairs?"

"Where else, Tex? It sure as hell ain't out in the alley." She leaned against his side, her plump hand dutifully groping for his crotch.

He turned slightly away from her and finished his beer. "I been where they was just tents out back in an alley."

"This is civilization, Tex. We got class here. J. T. Roebuck sees to that. The question is, have you got the price of a lady in those tight britches of yours?"

"How much?"

"Two dollars, Tex. And worth every cent."

"I'm sure of that, Sadie." Longarm finished his beer and wiped his mouth off with the back of his hand. Slamming down the empty glass, he grinned at her. "Let's go."

"My, oh my! Ain't we the eager one!"

"Been on the trail awhile. Ain't seen a woman since Texas."

She smiled coquettishly. "I *knew* you was from Texas. I can always tell. Just follow me, darlin'."

She took Longarm's hand and pulled him through the crowd and up the stairs. Once on the balcony, he confirmed what Doc Farnsworth had told him. The door to Roebuck's office was guarded by a lean gunman, who at the moment was leaning back on a wooden chair, a Greener across his lap.

As Sadie began to pull Longarm in the other direction along the balcony, Longarm reached out and caught her gently. She turned to look at him in some irritation.

"What's the matter, Tex?"

"I'd rather be in that room over there," he told her, indicating a room next to Roebuck's office. "The one facing front. Can't we use that one?"

"That ain't my crib, darlin'."

"Then I'm not interested. Forget it."

She was startled. Her bleary eyes looked up at him in sudden alarm. She had been so sure of him only a moment ago. Not it was all flying out the window. A hint of suppressed anger flared momentarily in her eyes. "But, Tex . . . !"

"I can't help it," Longarm said. "I was in a fire once—a big saloon like this one. What saved me was I could get out onto the roof facing the main street."

She frowned, then shrugged wearily, no longer angry, calculating how best to handle this strange, oversized Texan. "Well . . . I know the girl who uses that room," she told him uncertainly. "Maybe we can use it. But it'll cost you double, Tex."

"How much?"

"Two dollars for me—and two dollars for her. Her name is Irene."

"Sure. That's all right."

"And another dollar to me—for the aggravation," she finished boldly.

"That's pretty steep, ain't it?"

"Take it or leave it," the girl said sharply. She was no longer so anxious to please, it seemed. It had obviously been a long day.

"All right," Longarm said, digging into his jacket pocket.

He dropped the coins into her hand.

"C'mon," she told him.

Taking his arm possessively, she pulled him past the sleepy-eyed deputy outside Roebuck's door, obviously anxious to make sure Longarm would present her with no more surprises. Once at her fellow worker's door, she knocked lightly, then leaned her head against one of the panels.

"Irene . . . !" she called softly.

Longarm heard bedsprings creaking. The door opened a crack. Longarm could see the spill of dark hair and a pale chin.

"You takin' a break, Irene?" Sadie asked.

The voice that answered was furry with fatigue. "Yeah, Sadie. What is it?"

Sadie glanced at Longarm. "Tex here is afraid of fires. He wants a room near a roof. We was hoping we could use yours."

"Sure, but only with me in it," she told Sadie, pulling the door open wider to get a better look at Longarm. There was a half-empty bottle of whiskey in her hand.

Sadie shrugged. "If you're sure you can handle him."

Irene smiled crookedly and looked back at Sadie. "Sure, Sadie. I can handle him." Then she glanced back at Longarm. "Full rates, Tex. Two dollars. Anything extra, it'll cost you more."

"He's got plenty," assured Sadie.

Satisfied, Irene stepped back, her shift falling open in what was intended as a seductive move designed to set Longarm off. Longarm thanked Sadie with a nod and stepped past her into Irene's room. Irene closed the door and turned to face him. She had already had too much to drink, but was obviously determined to do her best.

"What's this about you bein' afraid of fires, Tex?" she asked, stepping out of her shift and throwing it at the foot of her cot.

39

She stood unashamed before him, her breasts sagging toward her overlarge belly, her pubic patch untidy, her knees dimpled, and no ankles that Longarm could see. Never before had Longarm realized how pathetically vulnerable a naked woman could look.

He took her gently by the shoulders and urged her toward the cot. She sat down on it, her eyes looking up at him questioningly, a tiny hint of fear in them. Gently, he took the bottle from her and set it down on the nightstand. Then he kissed her softly, almost tenderly, on her whiskey lips. As he pressed her back onto the cot, he took her shift and covered her with it.

Her feelings were obviously hurt; didn't he want her?

"Hey, Tex," she demanded. "What're you up to?"

"I ain't afraid of fire, Irene," he explained softly.

She blinked up at him, trying to understand. "Then, why . . . ?"

"Listen to me, Irene. I don't want to hurt you. It is not you I am after. This room will give me access to Roebuck's office without my having to blast my way in past that deputy. I could flash my badge, but if I did that, Roebuck would stall and the local sheriff would make it impossible for me to do my job."

"Badge . . . ?"

"I'm a U.S. deputy marshal, Irene."

She blinked unhappily, almost fearfully, up at him. The whiskey fog was lifting from her brain and she was able to see things more clearly, it seemed. Shaking her head unhappily, she said, "I don't want to get involved."

"Then don't. Lie still here and let me go out this window."

"You won't hurt me?"

"Why should I do that? I'm a lawman."

"If Roebuck finds out . . . !"

"He won't. Not if you lie still here and let me go out this window." He placed the whiskey back into her hand.

Like a babe taking her mother's breast, she placed the neck of the bottle in her mouth and nodded obediently. He patted her on the shoulder and lifted the window sash. Stepping out onto the wet roof, he winced slightly as the rain struck him in the face. He glanced back into the room. Her eyes shut, Irene had tipped the bottle straight up and was gulping down the rest of the raw whiskey—determined, it seemed, to put herself out of it.

Crouching low behind the railing, Longarm made his way along the roof until he came to the window to Roebuck's office and looked in. The room was more than triple the size of the dingy crib he had just left, and there was a door leading to another room, indicating that Roebuck had a full suite of rooms up here The office was luxuriously appointed, with solid, well-upholstered leather chairs and a large sofa. Set against the far wall was a highly polished mahogany table and chairs. Over the table hung a large, gilt-framed mirror.

Two men were visible. J. T. Roebuck was at his desk with his back to Longarm. Tate Rawson—the man Longarm was now almost certain had goaded Clint Bolen into firing on Longarm—was asleep on the sofa, his face turned to the wall. Roebuck was

41

busy counting a stack of what looked like stock or bond issues. A strongbox was open on the desk beside him, each compartment stuffed with currency.

Tate Rawson's sixgun was in its gunbelt, hung over the back of one of the table's mahogany chairs. There was no sign of the sheriff or anyone else in the room.

Longarm tried the window. It was not locked. He slid the sash up silently for almost two feet before the dampness in the wood caused the sash to stick. Roebuck's head, his pale scalp showing through his thinning hair, was less than two feet from the window, and the sudden damp draft on the back of his neck caused him to look around suddenly. When he saw the muzzle of Longarm's .44 yawning open less than a foot from his face, his small, piggish eyes almost popped out of his head.

"Don't make an outcry, Roebuck," Longarm told him. "Just sit quiet, or this might go off."

Longarm eased himself into the room and moved to the side of Roebuck's desk. Roebuck's round face was growing darker by the moment, flushed with outrage at this intrusion. Keeping his .44 trained on Roebuck, Longarm backed to the chair where Rawson's gunbelt was hanging. He withdrew the Smith & Wesson from its holster and stuck it into his belt. Then he crossed over to the couch and raised his Colt high over Rawson's head.

"Tate!" Roebuck called in warning.

Tate woke instantly and started to turn his head just as Longarm's gunbarrel crashed down. The blow was a glancing one. Tate Rawson shook himself convulsively, not yet out. Longarm stepped back and brought the Colt down again in a quick, chopping motion. This time he caught Tate's skull squarely. The gunman slacked back onto the sofa's cushions, unconscious.

Glancing up, Longarm saw Roebuck pawing furiously through one of his desk drawers. As Roebuck pulled out a pearl-handled derringer, Longarm reached the desk and smashed his gunbarrel down on Roebuck's wrist. The wristbone's sickening snap was almost lost in Roebuck's agonized cry as the derringer spun across the top of the desk and landed on the carpet.

The door leading out to the balcony opened. Longarm had expected this and was already striding toward the door. As the deputy saw Longarm approaching with a leveled sixgun, he tried to pull the door shut. But Longarm yanked the door all the way open, grabbed the man's shoulder, and hauled him inside. Kicking the door shut behind the deputy, Longarm knocked the Greener out of his hand, then clipped him on the side of the head with his sixgun. Unconscious, the deputy slipped almost soundlessly to the thick carpet.

Longarm turned back to Roebuck. The man was close to tears as he held onto his shattered right wrist.

"You're that U.S. marshal from Denver!" he blurted incredulously. "The one Tate said Bolen killed."

"That's right, Roebuck. And you're the one behind Milt Grumman's death."

"It was Tate! He's the one killed that deputy."

"On your orders, Roebuck."

"Prove it," Roebuck sneered. "It's my word

43

against yours. Tate'll deny it, and I'll back him. You can't touch him—or me. Where are your witnesses? And just who do you think you're dealing with, anyway? I got friends in Washington! Powerful friends. Congressmen, senators—cabinet officials! They got as much at stake in the right-of-way for this railroad as I have."

Longarm did not doubt Roebuck. He knew the man was not exaggerating. For Longarm to attempt to bring Tate Rawson to trial would be worse than futile. Longarm could count on no justice from that quarter.

"Never mind that, Roebuck," Longarm said. "You have those Mormon documents."

"And what if I do?"

"I want them. Now."

"I don't know what you're talking about!"

"You want me to break that other wrist?"

"You're a lawman! You wouldn't do that. It wouldn't be legal!"

Longarm's bark of laughter cut through Roebuck's bleat. "You're beyond the law now, Roebuck," Longarm reminded him. "And right now, the only law that matters is in my right fist. Give me those Mormon papers!"

"They're in my safe. You broke my hand. I can't open it."

"Use your left hand."

Roebuck looked desperately over at the still unconscious Rawson, hoping for a miracle of some kind. Then he looked back at Longarm and found no comfort in Longarm's cold, relentless eyes.

"All right," he told Longarm, his voice surly. "All right. But I'll need a minute."

"That's all I'm giving you."

Roebuck gave up then, and still holding his broken wrist, he hurried past Longarm over to the gilt-edged mirror and swung it away from the wall. There was a wall safe behind it. Swiftly he spun the safe's dial. The tumblers clicked softly; then Roebuck pulled open the safe and stepped aside. Longarm reached in and found two loosely bound books, each about the size of a family Bible, the covers made of heavy cardboard, the pages yellowing from age. He took both of them from the safe.

"Take off your frock coat, Roebuck."

It was painful for Roebuck to pull his broken wrist through the sleeve, but he managed, grimacing painfully.

Longarm wrapped the Mormon archives in the coat to protect them from the rain, then shoved them under his left arm and started for the window.

"Damn you, Marshal! You won't get away with this!"

"Won't I?" Longarm asked, pushing the window sash higher.

"Do you know how much money I got, you sonofabitch? I can buy and sell you three times over! I own this state—and everyone in it!"

"You don't own me—or the law."

"Yes, I do, you sonofabitch!" Seeing Longarm was getting ready to flee, Roebuck's blustering fury returned. "You'll see! That chief of yours in Denver will hear about this. I swear! If it's the last thing I do, I'll have your badge. You'll end up in prison if you ever show your face again in a federal marshal's office!"

Pausing, Longarm stared coldly back at the man. "What are you going to do, Roebuck? Complain to the authorities that I stole the records you stole from the Mormons?"

"The Mormons! Them stinkin' bigamists! We won't ever let them into the Union! You think anyone cares what happens to them crazies? You think *they* got clout!"

As far as Longarm was concerned, the argument was over. Holding onto the sash with his left hand, he poked his left leg out onto the roof.

"Just stay away from this window, Roebuck," Longarm warned. "I'll shoot the first one I see. From this roof it's an easy drop to the alley floor. I got a fast horse waiting for me. You'll never cut my sign in this rain. So don't even try."

"You're worse than a fool, lawman!" Roebuck snarled, his voice raw now with fury, "if you think I'll forget this! There's no place on earth where you can hide from me. If the law don't get you, Tate Rawson will! He'll track you clear to hell—and beyond, if need be."

"Fine," Longarm said. "Tell him I'll be waiting."

His .44 still trained on Roebuck, Longarm ducked his head under the sash. As he was pulling his other leg out after him, he glimpsed Tate Rawson leaping onto the floor behind Roebuck's desk. Using Roebuck's dropped derringer, Tate got off a shot, shattering the glass inches behind Longarm's head.

Longarm fired wildly back, shattering the windowpane and sending both men scurrying. Then he put his head down and darted back along the roof to Irene's room. Ducking through the open window, he closed it and turned to see Irene, flat on her back, the empty whiskey bottle on the floor beside her. Her mouth was open and she was snoring. He covered her up and stepped to the door to listen.

All hell was breaking loose. The sudden detonations just over the saloon had been more than enough to alert those below. Shouts came from the saloon. Booted feet thundered up the stairs to the balcony. Men were shouting out orders. There was a confused babble. Then, abruptly, above the commotion came Roebuck's furious bleat.

"Dammit, Sheriff!" screamed the man. "Don't let him get away! He robbed me. Get after him. He dropped into the alley. He's got a horse waitin'!"

A voice Longarm assumed belonged to Sheriff Tuttle began issuing orders, and Longarm could hear the men thundering back down the stairs, while still others pounded back up through the crush. The ruckus outside Roebuck's door increased. Calling out loudly for Doc Farnsworth's assistance, Roebuck ducked back into his office. Through the walls of Irene's room, Longarm could hear Roebuck berating the sheriff and Tate Rawson. Longarm glanced down at the girl. She was still on her back, still snoring.

Longarm waited patiently. The commotion on the balcony faded, while below in the street he could hear horses galloping away from the saloon, then cutting into the alley after him. Shouting, agitated men poured from the saloon, their disturbance enough to cut off the sound of the hard-charging horses.

Longarm snugged his hat tightly down over his forehead, then shifted the Mormon records more firmly up under his left arm and opened the door to peer out. A burly gent, wearing only the bottoms of his red longjohns, was standing at the balcony railing, peering down at the saloon in some annoyance. Stepping from the room, Longarm closed the door behind him. The door to the next crib was open. A girl was standing in the doorway, staring with some impatience at the man leaning on the balcony. All she was wearing was a knitted shawl she had thrown over her shoulders.

The fellow at the railing turned to Longarm.

"What's all the commotion?" Longarm demanded unhappily.

"Someone robbed J. T. Roebuck! Broke his arm, too!"

"That so?" Longarm shook his head, then winked at the man. "Well, the next time, I hope they wait until I'm finished." He indicated with a nod the room he had just left. "Know what I mean?"

"Sure do, mister!"

"If you do, get back in here," the girl in the doorway told him. "Your time is nearly up!"

With a nervous giggle, the fellow in the red longjohns padded happily back into the room. The door slammed shut and Longarm kept going, past Roebuck's office and on down the balcony. He descended the stairs calmly, without hurrying. When he reached the saloon floor, he found it deserted, except for the piano player who was idly picking out a sentimental tune on the piano.

As Longarm walked past him, he glanced up. "I hear someone knocked Roebuck around some."

"That's what I heard too," Longarm replied.

"Did they get that bastard Tate Rawson?"

"I don't think so."

"Shit," the piano player said, turning back to his keyboard.

Longarm stepped out through the batwings, hunched his shoulders against the rain, and hurried across the street through the milling crowd to the alley that ran alongside the livery stable. A moment later he slipped silently in through a small rear door he had noticed earlier.

The rain thundering on the livery roof helped muffle his footsteps as he approached the hostler from behind. The old cowpoke was doing precisely what Longarm had expected him to do. He had taken Longarm's Winchester from its scabbard and hunkered down behind a couple of barrels to wait for Longarm to step through the open door. Halting behind the wrangler, Longarm rested the barrel of his .44 against the back of his head. The man groaned softly and dropped the Winchester.

"Stand up, old man."

The hostler stood up and raised both hands over his head.

"Take off your boots, then your socks," Longarm told him. "And do it fast. I'm in kind of a hurry."

The old man kicked off his boots and peeled his stockings off. Stuffing one of the socks into the old man's mouth, Longarm wrapped the other sock around his mouth, knotting it at the back of his head. Then he took down some rope from the wall and

49

wound it around the old man, binding him securely, after which he pushed him into the feed room and dropped a peg through the latch.

He picked up his rifle and put it back into its scabbard. Then, opening one of his saddlebags, he discarded Roebuck's frock coat and placed the two Mormon record books inside it. A moment later, ducking his head low, he rode out of the livery into the slanting rain. He was wearing his slicker, and his hat brim was pulled well down over his face.

Ahead of him he saw horsemen milling about in front of the Lucky Lady. Some of the riders were shouting at men standing on the sidewalk, and those on the sidewalk were shouting advice to the men on horseback. Roebuck's fury had set them all in motion. But the plunge down the alley after Longarm had proved fruitless. Now the men did not know which direction Longarm had taken, and they were left to ride about aimlessly, hoping for someone to tell them which way to go.

As Longarm clopped steadily through the rain toward them, he heard shots behind him. They were coming from the other end of town. Distant shouts erupted soon after, followed by the sound of more firing. At once the milling horsemen in front of the Lucky Lady spurred their mounts past Longarm. As they headed toward the gunfire, they let loose with wild yells of anticipation, their guns gleaming in the rain.

His head low, the rain lashing at him, Longarm kept on past the Lucky Lady and headed out of town. He was almost across the wooden bridge when a horse and rider appeared from behind a clump of willows on the other side of the stream. A rifle poked out from under his slicker.

"Hold it, mister," the rider called, as Longarm finished crossing the bridge and gained the other side. "Just who might you be and where you goin'?"

Longarm didn't reply and didn't slow his horse. He had ridden the length of Ridge City's main street with his .44 resting in readiness on his right thigh. But he did not want to shoot. The gun's detonation would bring a storm of horsemen as surely as those other shots had. Longarm kept on moving toward the rifle-toting deputy.

"Name's Goodman," Longarm told him cheerfully. "Silas Goodman."

"Where're you goin'?"

"I'm getting out of this Godless town. It's gone plumb wild. Middle of the night and men are riding up and down the streets shoutin' like it was the Fourth of July."

"Yeah. Well, maybe you better pull up like I said." The rider pulled his horse around so that he was riding alongside Longarm. "I got orders to let no one out of town until we check 'im out."

"Orders? Whose orders?"

"Sheriff Tuttle. Now you just—"

Longarm swung his gunbarrel around, stopping the man in mid-sentence as it crashed into his face and knocked him back off his horse. The deputy landed heavily, but the ground was muddy enough to cushion his fall. Scrambling to his feet, he drew his sidearm. Longarm flung himself off his horse and grabbed the deputy's gun hand. The two went crash-

51

ing to the ground and began a desperate, silent struggle for possession of the weapon.

There was a muffled explosion. Longarm felt something hot and powerful plow into his right thigh with the numbing impact of a hard punch. Wresting the gun from the deputy's hand, Longarm brought it around, slamming him on the side of his head. Groaning, the deputy rolled over in the mud, then pushed himself doggedly up onto his hands and knees, his head sagging forward. Reaching over, Longarm grabbed his hair, pulled his face up, and punched him on the point of his jaw with all the force still at his command. The deputy flipped backward into the mud, and this time he lay still. Despite the searing pain growing in his thigh, Longarm managed to drag the deputy off the trail and into the clump of willows.

Mounting up was not easy as he dragged his right thigh over the cantle, then settled back painfully into the saddle. Reaching over, he took hold of the reins to the deputy's horse, then spurred his dun into the cold, wet night, pulling the deputy's mount after him. He did not want the riderless horse galloping back into Ridge City to alert Roebuck's men. Longarm needed time to put distance between himself and any pursuit so he would have time to get his wound looked after. Then he would find a Wells Fargo Express office and send the Mormon records to Billy Vail in Denver.

But that would not be the end of it—not for him.

There was still Clint Bolen to be dealt with. And if Longarm could count on Roebuck's grim threat,

Tate Rawson would catch up to him soon enough, presenting him with the opportunity no court of law would allow—the chance to execute the man who had killed Milt Grumman.

Then he would come back for J. T. Roebuck.

Chapter Four

Sheriff Tuttle and Tate Rawson watched as Doc Farnsworth finished putting on Roebuck's cast. Roebuck had been half out of his mind with the pain, and so wild and abusive was he that Farnsworth had had a difficult time setting the broken wristbone. Roebuck carried on as if the doctor and the others were personally responsible for the terrible pain he was being forced to endure.

At last Farnsworth stepped back and wiped his plaster-covered hands dry on a towel. Roebuck glanced from his cast to the doctor, a surly scowl on his face.

"It still hurts, Doc. Burns! Burns like hell!"

"And it will for a while. You've got to expect that."

"Well, dammit, what've you got for the pain?"

The doctor dropped the towel onto Roebuck's desk and poked about in his black bag. "All I have is some laudanum," he replied, lifting out a small pint bottle filled with tincture of opium.

"I don't want that snake oil, Doc. You mean that's all you got?"

"That's all."

"That stuff's addictin', ain't it?"

"Not if you're careful."

"It's addicting, then."

"I told you, J. T. Not if taken with discretion."

"What the hell's that supposed to mean? Half my girls are on that stuff and they can't get along without it. They use it for fleabite, stomach bile, insomnia. . . ."

The doctor shrugged and placed the bottle down on Roebuck's desk, then closed his bag and stepped back, anxious to get out of Roebuck's office and away from his irascible patient. A girl entered to take away the basin of water the doctor had used to moisten the plaster bandages. As she left with the basin, Farnsworth opened the door for her, bid Roebuck a hasty goodbye, and fled the room.

"That damned quack!" Roebuck snarled as the door closed behind him. "We ought to run him out of town."

Then he snatched the laudanum off the desk with his left hand and removed the cork with his teeth. Spitting it across the room, he took a hefty belt of the bitter concoction. Wiping his mouth with the back of his hand, he turned on Tate Rawson, his small, dark eyes glittering with suppressed fury.

"I want him, Tate. I want that fool deputy marshal. Bring his scalp back to me so I can nail it to the wall. Is that clear?"

"You meant that? His *scalp?*"

"What's the matter. Something wrong with your hearing?"

Sheriff Tuttle cleared his throat unhappily. "See here, J. T.," he began, "why not let me handle this deputy for you? Just let me speak to a few boys in the capital, and we can have him in no time."

"No, dammit! Leave him to Tate."

"But, J. T., that's not lawful. We got to be sure we—"

"Lawful! Damn you, Tuttle! It's you and your deputies let that sonofabitch sneak out of here right under your noses. Get out of here, Tuttle. You're good enough to collar drunks and troublemakers, but that deputy needs a finer hand."

Unhappy, the sheriff began to twirl his hat nervously. He disliked being dismissed in this manner, but did not know how to prevent it. He glanced miserably at Tate Rawson.

"Go on!" Roebuck repeated. "You heard me, Tuttle. Get out of here. If I want you for anything, I'll let you know."

"But J. T.—"

"Tate! Throw this fat slob out of here!"

Crestfallen, the big man clapped his big white hat on and fled to the door. Grinning malevolently, Roebuck waited until the sheriff had vanished out the door before he looked back at Tate Rawson.

"You too, Tate. I want you to get on this. Get after that bastard."

"Now?"

"Yes! Now! You were supposed to have killed this deputy. What happened?"

"Like I told you. I let Bolen take care of it. He was just a lousy shot, I guess. It was raining pretty hard. Last we saw, the deputy was being swept under water. The sonofabitch must have as many lives as a cat."

"Well, see to it that he doesn't have any more."

"I'll need a good horse—and a stake."

Roebuck opened a drawer, reached in clumsily with his left hand, and withdrew a thick wad of bank notes held together with a rubber band. He tossed the wad across the desk at Tate.

"There's a thousand there," he said. "Come back with that deputy's badge and his scalp and there'll be another thousand waiting. Come back with Bolen's deed to the spread I signed over to him and there'll be another thousand."

"Hell, J. T., I'd have to kill Bolen to get that."

"You think I don't know that? Now that the cat's out of the bag, it won't be very smart for either of us to let Clint Bolen live. He could maybe make things hot for both of us one day."

"What about the girl?"

Roebuck's eyes gleamed. "Do what you want with her."

Pleased, Rawson nodded quickly and swept up the bills. "Two scalps," he said, grinning, "at one thousand each. Them's damn good prices, J. T."

"Just see you earn it, Tate. I want both men dead."

"You got it."

"Go on out to the ranch. Tell them I told you to

give you that big chestnut, the one with the blaze on its forehead. It's big and it's strong. Get after that bastard, Tate."

"I heard you, J. T."

Rawson hurried to the door and left. As the door closed behind him, Roebuck glanced down at the cumbersome cast enclosing his wrist and swore bitterly. Then he grabbed the bottle of laudanum and took another healthy belt of the dark, pungent liquid.

He began to chuckle, remembering the unhappy look on Tuttle's face when he chased him from the room. Then he began to laugh out loud, feeling all of a sudden much better—and took another long pull on the laudanum.

Longarm did not go straight north to Pine Ridge. Assuming that Tate Rawson would be close behind him and that he needed time to recoup, he cut northwest, following the bed of a stream for a full day to throw Tate off. Deep now in the western reaches of the Salmon River Mountains, he halted on a ridge. He had caught sight of a mine entrance below him.

As he watched, a lone woman appeared, pushing a loaded wheelbarrow from the mine. Below the mine the flow from a spring had been diverted onto a wooden trough connected to a large cradle. Using a wooden ramp that sagged precariously under her, she gained the platform alongside the cradle and dumped the ore into it. Then, diverting the water into the trough, she began rocking the cradle to isolate the gold-bearing ore from the slag, busily plucking out and tossing aside the largest chunks of worthless ore.

Unaware of him watching from the ridge, she worked steadily, head down, intent on her labor. On her head she wore a large, black, floppy-brimmed hat, and her long skirts brushed the platform as she bent over the cradle. Towering over her and set starkly against the wall of sheer rock behind it were the broken weathered remnants of a stamping mill. The tin roof had been peeled off by the wind, and the mill's skeletal structure was now visible through the gaping holes in its sides.

By this time Longarm was aware that his wound was more serious than he had realized at first. He needed a place where he could lie low for a while until he had recovered enough to continue on to Pine Ridge. There was about this woman below him the unmistakable air of one who was completely alone, doggedly making do on her own. He wondered if he should prevail upon her to take him in. A tall, raw-boned woman—almost fifty, he judged—it was not likely she would develop any romantic attachment to him; and this made her seem eminently suitable for his purposes. Still, he disliked dragging an innocent bystander into the web of events now threatening to ensnare him.

Longarm sat his dun a while longer, watching the woman as she left the cradle and pushed the empty wheelbarrow back into the mine. When she vanished into the tunnel's dark maw, he turned his mount and rode on into the thick stand of timber covering the mountainside before him. He had better keep going and not bother this solitary toiler, he told himself. Perhaps before nightfall he would find an empty line shack where he could hole up.

But what he found before long was that he could no longer sit a horse. Forced to dismount or fall from the saddle, he eased himself carefully down off the dun and led it from the timber. As he stepped out onto a shelf of bedrock, he saw a cabin on the other side of a narrow gully, perched precariously on a small rise. He was able to catch the bright gleam of a curtain in one of the windows and realized the cabin probably belonged to the woman he had seen working the mine.

He turned away, intending to move back into the timber until he was past the cabin. But he was too weak for that and sat heavily down on a flat boulder to wait for the world to stop spinning about him. A twig snapped behind him. He turned his head and saw the woman emerging cautiously from the timber toward him, a Winchester in her hand.

"Waitin' up here to rob me, are you?" she demanded, leveling the rifle at him. "Thought I didn't see you!"

Longarm shook his head wearily. "I wasn't waiting to rob you," he told her, careful not to make any sudden movements. He had no way of knowing how nervous she was, or how skilled in handling the Winchester.

"You expect me to believe that?" she demanded coldly. "A decent, honest man would have made himself known to me—would have called out."

"Maybe so," he admitted.

"Then why didn't you?"

"I suppose I should have," Longarm said, his head still reeling dangerously. "But I didn't want—"

The woman spun onto her head and the sky

61

flipped under her, and he felt himself falling. The back of his head struck something cold and unyielding—the caprock. Flashing lights exploded deep inside his skull. Then the bright sky and the upside down woman winked out as darkness claimed him.

When he regained consciousness, he was in a bed inside the cabin, the woman bent over him, her strong, raw-boned face grim, her large dark eyes narrowed with concern.

"How'd you get me in here?" he asked.

She pulled back. A brief smile played over her face. "I used the wheelbarrow."

"Serves me right."

"I took a bullet out of your thigh."

"Thanks."

"Then I washed it good and proper with soap and water. You should be all right."

"Since when is soap and water good for gunshot wounds?"

"Soap and water is good for everything. This is a dirty world. That's where all our trouble comes from."

Longarm was too tired to argue. He let his head turn to the wall and darkness came a second time.

Less than a week later Longarm found himself sitting outside the cabin on a battered wooden chair, the late afternoon sun gently toasting him. The woman—her name was Patricia Fields—was not yet back from the mine, and he had been left as usual to his own devices. During this past week, he had slept almost continuously, awakening only long enough, it seemed, to consume hot broth and soup. He had had as yet only the most rudimentary conversations with the woman. But he knew her name and assumed she had found his identity when she examined his wallet.

This was the first day he had felt strong enough to dress and go outside. He felt a lot lighter—and was. But he walked without pain now, and knew it would not be long before he was able to ride out.

She arrived back up on her mule, dismounted, and led the animal into the small shed behind the cabin. A moment later she reappeared and, brushing her hands, walked toward him, squinting through the low sun at him.

"I see you're up," she said by way of greeting.

"Yes, thanks to you."

"You have a fine, powerful constitution—or you would never gotten as far as you had with that bullet in you." She pulled up beside him, her arms akimbo. "You hungry?"

"I could eat a bear."

"Hang in there. It won't be long."

"The bear?"

She smiled and shook her head. "No. Beans and flapjacks and coffee. The same old fare."

"Don't knock it."

She turned and disappeared into the cabin, then came for him a few minutes later. He protested that he did not need assistance, and got up from the chair and walked back into the cabin under his own steam. She seemed pleased at his progress.

His meal was waiting for him on a well-scrubbed plank table, an oversized mug of black coffee sitting

63

beside his plate. The flapjacks were stacked high and there was plenty of honey. She sat down across from him and looked closely at his face.

"You look pale," she said. "You sure you want to stay up?"

"I'm pale because I'm hungry," he said, reaching for the jar of honey.

As he spread it liberally over the flapjacks, she said, "I looked through your things and found that badge. Your name is Custis—Custis Long. And you're a lawman."

"That's right, ma'am."

"My friends used to call me Pat."

"Don't they still do that?"

"My friends are all dead. Like my husband. What he left me was this mine, and that's all. I'm workin' it and making do."

"My friends call me Longarm."

She nodded and for a while they ate in silence. Downing the flapjacks and beans, Longarm soon felt better, the coffee doing much to perk him up.

When she poured him his second cup, she said, "You are after someone. A man called Tate."

He looked at her, frowning. He had not recalled telling her that.

She filled her own mug. "You had a fever. You talked a lot. At times I had to hold you down. You mentioned this man Tate often."

With a shrug he described Rawson to her carefully so she would recognize him if he ever showed up; then he told her about the Mormon chronicles and what had followed when he had found Milt Grumman dead in that wagon.

64

"Tate Rawson's a killer," Longarm warned in conclusion. "If he shows up here on my trail, don't trust him."

"I'll fill his ass full of lead," she assured him.

"I'm sorry you're involved. I did not intend it. That's why I pulled back off the ridge and kept going."

She smiled at him. "And I thought you were doing that so you could take me by surprise—not to protect me."

"Anyway, I'm glad you followed after me with that Winchester."

"I am too, Longarm."

"You must be pretty lonesome out here."

"Yes and no. What I've learned about people in my line of work hasn't made me so anxious to see them—not if I don't have to."

"Your line of work?"

"I ran a sporting house in Leadville. It was there I met my husband, Tad. I staked him and he struck it rich." Her eyes began to glow as she remembered. "And for a time that's what we were—very rich. Trips to Europe, a mansion, fancy carriages. For a while it was my wildest fancies come true." She smiled sadly. "It was surprising how soon we got used to having all that money—and then the mine was all played out and we had nothing."

"So you came back here alone?"

"First I tried to get back into my profession, but it was difficult to get the right girls, and my locations were always poor, it seemed. Besides, that can be a very depressing business at times."

"That's right," Longarm said. "No matter what the location or who runs the parlor."

She waited until Longarm finished his coffee before replying. It seemed important to her that she explain things to him. "I went into the sporting life because it was the only business a woman was allowed to own. And that's what it was—a business, pure and simple. I had no education, and I had no man to take care of me. My face has character now; it was just plain ugly then. It was a way for me to survive, and I did. Furthermore, I operated the best house in town." She smiled ironically. "My clients were some of the most important men in the West."

"I wasn't thinking of you. Or the men. I was thinking of the girls."

"I never took a girl in who was a virgin or inexperienced. That was a rule I never broke. Most of the girls that came to me had already run away from their husbands—or else they'd gotten involved with a man, then been abandoned. It was either the street and starvation for most of them, or my house. Hell, Longarm, some of my girls ended up married to my customers. And they made good wives, from all I've been able to gather. They understood a man's needs and knew how to pleasure him, and they were faithful to their husbands."

"You make your house sound like a school for wives."

She smiled. "Maybe that's what it was, Longarm. For some of them, anyway. It made me a good and loving wife to Tad. I never cheated on him. He was a good man and I loved him."

"He never brought up your past?"

"Never. Like I said, he was a good man—and a gentleman."

She got up then and proceeded to clear off the table. Longarm got up and stretched, his stomach full. Then he walked outside to get more of the sun. He felt like a young mud turtle discovering spring.

Longarm turned over in his cot, instantly awake. He could feel Pat standing beside him and realized she had bathed and scented herself with sweet grass. He himself had bathed by the stream before retiring, using a yellow bar of soap she had provided for him. The interior of the cabin was blacker than pitch, but even so, his eyes were gradually able to pick out the pale glow of her tall, naked form. In the darkness her pubic patch seemed to appear and disappear in the midst of shimmering paleness.

And then she knelt beside him.

"I am older than you, Longarm," she whispered. "But I am clean and free of disease. And I still know how to please a man."

"I'm sure you do, Pat."

She brushed her finger lightly over his face, and a moment later she was kissing him, softly at first, her head moving only slightly, her lips parting his with a gentleness that was close to a caress. Then she lifted her face away, turned her head, and rested her cheek against his.

"Was that the kiss of an old woman, Longarm?"

"No, Pat," Longarm told her, astonished. "It was not."

Swiftly yet lightly she lifted the sheet covering him and slipped in beside him. As he felt the warmth of her long limbs beside his, he realized how well she had kept herself. Undoubtedly, the work on the mine had done much to keep her in shape. Her breasts were still full, almost buoyant, as she held herself against him. He felt the fire in his loins leaping to life.

Her lips found his a second time. Again there was the gentleness, the delicious, practiced restraint. She teased him with the tip of her tongue. It was only for an instant. He enclosed her in his arms, moving hungrily over onto her. She pulled her mouth away from his and began to nibble his earlobe.

"Slow down, Longarm," she whispered. "There's no hurry!"

He chuckled, then moved his lips down past her chin and began kissing her neck. He heard her soft murmurs of pleasure and moved his lips still further down until he found her breasts. He could not believe their warmth. Under his questing mouth they became full, thrusting up at him, the nipples hardening. He toyed with them expertly, nipping at them lightly with the tips of his teeth, flicking at them with his tongue. She had tried to drive him to distraction by her deliberate lovemaking. But he was in charge now; she had ignited him completely. His lips moved down to her belly.

He felt her being caught up as well. What had been for her in the beginning simply an exercise in craft had rapidly become something more—much more.

He kissed her belly, moved down to her pubis, lingered there tantalisingly, then moved back to her breasts, crouching over her now, his erection pulsing almost painfully between his thighs. He heard her moan. He chuckled as she sank her teeth into his shoulder, biting almost hard enough to draw blood. He leaned quickly over her breasts, took one in his mouth, roughly. Groaning again, she spread herself to receive him, her legs raised high, her hips rolling and rising as he plunged finally deep into her. She was tight as a clenched fist.

"Slow," she whispered huskily, her head back, both arms flung about his neck. "That's it. Oh, so nice and slow. Yes . . . !"

Twice when he felt her nearing climax he slowed to a stop, plunging fully into her hot depths, holding himself still, pressing in as deeply as he could without motion. Each time, her breathing eased and her moans died away until he began thrusting again. At last she cried out, then began trembling from head to foot. She was ready now. Stepping up his tempo, he soon forgot her as he soared himself, bringing her with him to a final, shattering explosion that left them both limp and motionless.

After they regained their breath, Longarm rolled off her and she ran her fingers through his damp hair. "How soon before the encore?" she whispered huskily.

"My God," he moaned.

"I am insatiable, Longarm."

"I reckon so—if that means you can't get enough."

She laughed softly, her voice rich and warm, as if all her years had been wiped away in that flood of passion. "Yes. That's what it means. Do you blame me? How often will such an opportunity come again to an old woman?"

"You sure don't seem old, and that's the truth of it."

"Lovemaking does have a way of stopping time," she murmured, closing her eyes and breathing deeply. "Sometimes even rolling it back some."

Longarm rested his head between the lovely swell of her breasts. She put her arm around him and held him close against her warmth. The intoxicating smell of her lulled him. He felt his senses being swept away by delicious tides of sleep.

And then he became aware of her hands moving expertly over his limbs, exploring every secret part of him. She had shifted so that he was on his back under her, while she was on top of him, leaning her face over his, the moist tip of her tongue tracing his eyelids and ears, then trailing mischieviously down his cheek before it insinuated itself between his parted lips. Her warm hands had already brought him nearly erect again, and now, as her tongue darted wantonly into his mouth, he felt his erection peaking once more.

In that instant she leaned back and plunged down upon his shaft. Again and again she plunged down onto him. He heard her gasp, then her whimper, as she came, shuddering. Longarm clapped his big hands over her buttocks then, and kept her on top of him. He began thrusting up into her. She uttered a tiny little cry and arched herself back over his quivering, upthrusting body. His momentum increased. She hung on, delighted. At last she came to life again. Panting wildly, half shouting through gritted teeth, she rocked wildly, with an abandon that startled him. Groans broke from deep within her. She was riding him now with eyes squeezed shut, her hair a dark cloud billowing wildly about her head. Longarm reached for her breasts. Grabbing them both, he hung onto her as she rocked with demented abandon above him. Her groans became deeper and more full-throated, while Longarm continued his own wild, heedless upward surges. Her juices were flowing freely now, running down onto his belly and down his thighs as his calloused hands held her tightly down upon him.

Longarm felt himself moving swiftly beyond and then over the edge.

"Now!" she cried. "Oh, *now*. Longarm . . . !"

He felt her body tensing. She began to come then, in a long, shuddering climax as he continued to arch up under her. His hands clung to her fiercely as his own violent spasm wrenched him. Again and again he spent himself deep within her, exploding, gushing furiously. . . .

Panting softly, she sank down upon his chest and embraced him with her strong arms, hugging him close, not wanting to let him go, willing his erection to remain forever within her. But he realized achingly that there was no way she could do that.

He was strong and he was reasonably young and he was healthy, but he was not eternal.

After breakfast the next morning, Longarm went out to see to his dun. It was fat and sassy and needed to get some miles under its belt. When he left the shed, he saw Pat step from the cabin and head toward him. Their conversation at breakfast had been brief, shy almost. Now, as she came toward him, Longarm saw how her cheeks glowed and caught the clear sparkle in her dark eyes. *Hell, you feel pretty damn good yourself, old son,* he told himself. Pat stopped in front of him, a pleased smile on her face.

"How's the horse look?"

"Fat and sassy. Ready to move out."

"And what about you?"

"The same, I guess."

"How do you feel?"

"A damn sight better than when you carried me inside with a wheelbarrow. And for that I thank you, Pat."

"And thanks to you, I feel a lot better myself. No woman's the worse for having met you, Longarm."

"Thanks, and I'm much obliged for... everything, Pat."

"It was no chore."

She stayed with him while he saddled the dun. Having already anticipated his decision to leave, as soon as he mounted up she handed him beef sandwiches wrapped in shiny white butcher paper.

"Made the bread myself," she said.

He grinned. "I could smell it," he said, taking the sandwiches from her. Then he leaned low enough for her to kiss him on the lips. She stepped back afterward and squinted up at him, tears gleaming on her cheeks. He turned the dun and set off. When he was almost out of sight of the cabin, he glanced back. She was still standing in front of the cabin, watching him.

He waved. She waved back.

Then he put his horse on down the gentle slope before him, heading east now—toward Pine Ridge.

Chapter Five

A week before Longarm headed east for Pine Ridge, Clint Bolen sat in a hotel saloon, nursing a shotglass of whiskey. He had been sipping it for the past two hours. It was three o'clock in the afternoon, a dead time in the Cosmopolitan's saloon, perfect for his troubled reassessment of his dealings with J. T. Roebuck.

Slowly he turned his glass, considering every angle, aware that he had to do something unexpected or risk Roebuck's certain retaliation. Word had reached Clint that the deputy marshal he thought he had killed was alive and had taken the Mormon records back from J. T. With the deputy on the loose, Clint was now a danger to Roebuck. Clint knew too much. If that deputy ever caught up to him, Clint could implicate not only Tate Rawson in the murder of that other deputy, but Roebuck himself as its instigator.

But here in Pine Ridge Clint was smack in the middle of Roebuck land, dependent upon J. T. for everything—from water for his stock to the stock itself. Whenever he wanted, Roebuck could turn on Clint, and there would be nothing Clint could do about it. If he protested, a simple nod to Tate Rawson and Clint would be a dead man—and Clint could not be sure that Roebuck had not already given that fateful nod to his hired killer.

Unless . . .

Dudley Watts planted himself in front of Clint's table. The man was carrying a beer and was obviously intent on joining Clint. The night before Clint had met the man and had liked him well enough. Acting as point man for his brothers, Dudley Watts was looking for a spot to locate a good-sized cattle operation. The only thing that stood in the way of his accomplishing this was, of course, the Roebuck Land and Cattle Company, which held title to or controlled every water hole or creek in the valley clear to the Bitterroots.

Clint was not in the mood for Dudley Watts, or his simmering dislike of anything that had to do with the Roebuck Land and Cattle Company. But before Clint could say anything to dissuade the man, Watts slumped down at his table and smiled ruefully at Clint.

"My head's still spinning from last night," he confessed, "and my stomach wants to light out, seems like."

"Take some hair of the dog."

"That's just what I'm doin', Clint."

Clint forced himself to smile.

Dudley Watts was a powerful hulk of a man with nearly jet-black hair, thick strands of which poked out from under his wide-brimmed hat. Mats of thick, kinky hair covered the backs of his hands and surged up out of the open collar of his red woolen undershirt in a kind of exuberant lushness. His eyes seemed lit by a blue flame. The man was charged with a fierce, exultant vitality that spilled out into every move he made, every word he uttered. Even sitting down at the table across from Clint, Watts appeared to Clint as a surging force only momentarily capped, a dynamo at rest. Clint could not help wondering what his other four brothers were like. According to Watts, they were all bigger than he was.

Must be a tribe of grizzlies, Clint had commented to himself.

Clint picked up his whiskey and downed it. Slapping the glass back onto the table, he asked, "When are you expecting your brothers to get here, Watts?"

"They got here this morning. Right now they're camped just outside of town. We got too much gear to haul into town—plus all that cattle we're drivin'." The man shook his massive head dispiritedly. "Looks like we'll just have to keep on moving, though, through the Bitterroots and on into Montana."

"How much cattle you got?"

"Close to two thousand head."

"Jesus. That's some herd."

Dudley Watts nodded happily. "It's all we got in the world, Clint. Our life savin's is sunk in that stock."

Clint frowned and pulled back for a moment in his chair, regarding Dudley Watts in a sudden, new light. And in that instant he knew what he was going to do. Damn! If it wasn't strange the way things worked out! What was it that had made this hulking giant pick him out for a drinking companion the night before—and sit down at his table now? Whatever it was, it was going to change their lives.

"Dudley," Clint said carefully, peering intently into the big man's eyes, "how would you like to own the nicest spread south of the Salmon River? There's plenty of water, and unbroken range clear to the Bitterroots."

Dudley Watts pushed his hat back off his forehead to peer more carefully at Clint. "What in hell . . . ? Ain't that the spread this side of Roebuck's Circle R?"

"It is. And I've got Roebuck cattle to stock it with."

"Then what're you doin' selling it to me?"

"That's my business."

Watts rubbed his huge hand over the stubble on his chin. The raw, scratching sound it made could be heard clear to the bar. "You sayin' you'd sell?"

"For the right price."

"You got the deed?"

"I got the deed—and the land office is still open."

"How much?"

"What were you planning on paying?"

Watts' eyes got suddenly crafty. "Two thousand."

"Four."

"Three thousand and that's tops."

"Cash?"

"If you got the title, I got the cash. It's in the hotel safe."

"You haven't seen the land yet."

"Yes, I have. That was the first spread I looked at. The buildings are all good. The corrals are in repair, and its got just about the nicest, sweetest grass in this valley."

Clint nodded a bit regretfully. It was indeed a fine spread, and he was not very happy with having to let it go like this. "If you've seen the land and the buildings and you like it, then it's a deal, Watts."

The two shook on it.

Anxious to get his money and hightail it to the land office, Watts started to get out of his seat. Clint held him back with an upraised palm.

"Hold it a minute, Dudley. There's maybe a few jokers in the deck."

The big man sat down warily. "What is it, Clint?"

"You already know most of it. You'll have to contend with Roebuck and his hardcases. His holdings are all around you. And he has first call on the water rights. Roebuck's a big man in this state, and he never figured to let anyone but me take that spread."

"Why?"

"Can't you guess?"

"Because he can make you dance to his tune."

"Precisely."

"So if you sell to us, you'll be crossin' him."

"Yes—and I'll be putting you and your brothers squarely in the middle."

"Shit. We can handle that bastard."

It was the response Clint had hoped for—but he

had another joker left to pull out of the deck. "There's one more thing, Watts."

"I'm listening."

"There might be a man on my trail—a killer. He works for Roebuck. I don't know for sure, but I got an itchy feeling."

"Looks like you're interested in burning some bridges behind you."

Clint nodded grimly. "You could put it that way."

"Is that it, Clint? That all the jokers you got left to play?"

Clint nodded.

Watts grinned hugely and leaned back in his chair. "Hell, Clint! You give us clear title to that spread and we'll take on the king of England—let alone that tinhorn Roebuck and his hired guns. Me and my brothers'll make mincemeat out of the Circle R and the whole damned lot of 'em. Don't you worry none about that."

"Then it's a deal?"

Dudley Watts got to his feet, leaving his forgotten stein of beer on the table. "You're goddamn right it's a deal. We shook on it, remember? Now let's get on down to that land office before it closes."

Clint hurried after Watts and waited as the big man stopped at the hotel's front desk and asked for the money he had stashed in the hotel safe. While he waited, he wondered how Melissa would take this sudden change in their plans.

Later that same afternoon Clint knocked once on the door to their room, then turned the knob and entered. Melissa was sitting by the window, dressed in her rose dress—the one he liked so much—her hands folded in her lap. At his entrance, she turned hopefully, her eyes lighting up. She was expecting to leave for the ranch at any moment, he knew, and his heart sank at the prospect of telling her what he had just done.

"Who was that man, Clint?"

He stopped. "What man?"

"The one I saw you leave the hotel with earlier."

He had forgotten that she would have been at the window, looking out, that she could not have missed seeing him crossing the street with Watts.

"That was Dudley Watts."

"Did you hire him?"

"No, Mel."

"I thought you were looking for a foreman."

"I already hired another man. Petey Martin."

"Oh."

He sat down on the edge of the bed and cleared his throat. "Mel, I got something to tell you."

She looked at him with sudden apprehension. "What is it, Clint?"

"I sold the ranch for three thousand."

She frowned. "What?"

"You heard me, Mel. I sold the spread. I got three thousand for it."

For a long moment she looked at him without speaking. "I don't understand, Clint. Aren't we going out there tomorrow? Isn't that why you hired a foreman?"

"I need the foreman I hired to help us drive our cattle west—into Oregon. He'll help us find a place there, Mel."

"Oregon?" By this time she was completely bewildered.

"Yes."

"But Clint . . . Oregon? My god, *why?*"

He told her what he had learned the night before, that a deputy U.S. marshal had cornered Roebuck in his office and retrieved the Mormon chronicles they had given him. He did not tell Melissa of his bungled attempt to kill this same deputy earlier.

"Where did you hear this?"

"Tim Prewitt. He rode into town from the Circle R last night. I saw him at the bar downstairs."

"So now Mr. Roebuck doesn't have the records I took?"

"Not anymore."

She took a deep breath. "I see."

"It's all coming unraveled, Mel," he told her. "I don't like it. Roebuck is liable to come after me."

"But why? It's not your fault what happened."

"Yes. Mel. In a way, it is."

"I don't understand."

"Just take my word for it, will you, Mel? The thing is, this changes everything."

"But why should it?"

"Don't you see? While Roebuck had them Mormon records, we had a hold on him. Now, as far as those land deeds and rights of way are concerned, he's right back where he started from."

"All right, Clint. But that's *his* problem. We don't want to build any railroad."

He took a deep breath. "Mel, with Roebuck no longer pulling strings for us, the law can catch up to us any time. Don't forget. We stole those documents.

Fact is, I think that same deputy might be on our trail this very minute."

"He's after us?"

"Yes, Mel."

She shuddered as the realization of this new peril swept over her. "Oh, Clint!" Tears burst from her eyes.

He got up from the bed and knelt by her chair. Taking her in his arms, he soothed her as best he could, kissing her tenderly and stroking her long hair. "I didn't mean to frighten you, Mel. But now you know why I sold out. Only don't worry, Mel. I know of a hidden valley. There's plenty of room for us, it's lush, a perfect place."

"How far is it?"

He took a deep breath. "No sense in denying it, Mel. It'll be a long haul."

"But will we be safe there?"

"I hope so. At least we'll have the cattle to start us off—and plenty of folding money. We'll make it, Mel. Don't you worry none about that."

She wiped her eyes quickly, chastened. "I'm sorry I let go like that, Clint. It's just that all this comes so suddenly."

He smiled, relieved she was taking it so well. He leaned forward and kissed her lightly on the forehead. "I know, Mel. I understand. But do bear up, please. I'm counting on you, don't forget."

She nodded quickly, eagerly. "And I'm counting on you, too."

He stood up and took her in his arms. She flung her arms about his neck and melted into him. As he carried her over to the bed, he tried to think only of how good she smelled and how much he loved her, but since the night before all he had been able to think about was that deputy Prewitt had told him about—and Roebuck's killer, Tate Rawson.

He couldn't help himself.

Early the next morning Clint purchased a large supply wagon, loaded it up past the sideboards with provisions, then rode out of town with Melissa. At noon he returned alone on a saddle horse and joined his new foreman, who was waiting for him on the hotel porch. The two men rode out to the Circle R and pulled up in front of the large main house. Dismounting, Clint greeted Tim Prewitt, who was standing on the verandah.

"Come for your cattle?" the Circle R foreman asked him.

"That's right, Prew."

Prewitt pointed to a long meadow stretching beyond the main horse barn. It was speckled with cattle. "Most of them's yours. You got the bill of sale Roebuck gave you?"

Climbing the verandah steps, Clint unfolded the letter Roebuck had given him and handed it to Prewitt. The foreman studied it judiciously. "Yep. That's the old bastard's hand, all right," he said, giving it back to Clint.

"I'd like five mounts, as well."

"That letter don't say nothin' about horseflesh."

"Take it out of the cattle."

The foreman shrugged, then descended the porch steps and peered up at Petey Martin, his square, blocky face creasing into a grin. "Hello, Petey. Sick of loafin', hey?"

Clint's foreman smiled down at Prewitt, the lines of his leathery face stretching tautly. His smile was honest, the eyes steady. "I guess you could say that, Prew."

Prewitt looked back at Clint. "Pick out the horses you want. I figure it'll cost you twenty-five head."

"I say fifteen."

Prewitt squinted at Clint and rubbed his palm over his stubbly chin. "Twenty, Clint. I'm doin' this on my own, and I don't want to lose my job."

"All right. Twenty head."

"You takin' the herd today?"

"That's what we're here for."

"Just you two going to drove 'em?"

"We aren't going that far," pointed out Clint. "Just to the head of the valley. Won't take more than a couple of days."

"Yeah, I suppose. All right. Let's go pick out them horses."

Petey dismounted to join them, and the three men trudged across the yard toward the big barn.

It was hot, dusty work cutting out the four hundred head, but Clint and Petey were finished by three o'clock and on their way. Clint was pleased with Petey's work, confident that with the help of a man as quietly competent as he was, Melissa and he would be able to make the long trek over the mountains.

He was careful to drive the cattle in a northeasterly direction until he was well out of sight of the

Circle R ranch buildings. Only when they were within a few miles of the spread he no longer owned did he drive the herd across a small tributary of the Salmon River and turn due west.

It was close to sundown by that time and fully dark before they reached a tableland deep inside the Salmon River range and kept climbing toward the distant peaks. Many miles further on, a campfire beckoned to them through the darkness, pulling them still higher. The cattle, footsore and weary by this time, protested, but Clint and Petey continued to drive them until at last they reached the stream-watered flat Clint had described to Melissa.

She was camped by the stream, waiting for them with a pot of coffee sitting on a flat stone by the campfire.

Clint introduced Melissa to Petey, who then downed a scalding cup of coffee, mounted up again, and rode out to quiet the herd and see that it was properly bedded down for the night. But the cattle were so exhausted, they dropped almost in their tracks and grew still. When the moon rose, Petey returned to the campfire for the food Melissa had prepared, while Clint took his place.

About four that morning, with the moon still casting a bright glow over the mountainside, Clint returned to the camp and approached Melissa, asleep in her bedroll under the wagon. He stopped a few feet from her and looked down at her tousled hair, noting the faint glow of moonlight on her pale cheek.

She stirred and opened her eyes, saw him standing there. Sitting up quickly, she looked at him.

"Join me," she told him. "We're married now, don't forget."

A wind blew down off one of the snow-capped peaks ringing them, chilling Clint. He hunkered down beside her and laid his palm against her cheek. "Get some sleep, Mel. You deserve it. You've done great, meeting us like this. But don't forget, we got a long haul ahead of us."

She nodded wearily and dropped back to her *soogan*, pulling the blanket up over her shoulders. He watched her for a while until he saw she was asleep. Then he left her and sat down beside the campfire's embers and built himself a cigarette. As he pulled the smoke into his lungs, he tried to throw off the chill that still held him. It had nothing to do with the wind coming off the peaks. It came from deep within him.

He told himself that one day he would make Melissa forget they were outlaws—that together, Melissa and he would build a new life for themselves on the other side of this range.

But he didn't really believe it.

Chapter Six

Three days after Clint Bolen vanished with his herd,
Longarm rode into Pine Ridge, turned down its main
street and left his mount at the livery across from the
Cosmopolitan Hotel. After checking into the hotel,
he walked to the Wells Fargo Express office, where
he sent off the Mormon chronicles to the U.S. marshal's office in Denver and a telegram to Billy Vail
advising him the package was on its way. Then he
asked the telegrapher where he could find the sheriff's office.

The sheriff was busy at his cluttered desk in the
corner of his office, the door leading to the cell block
open behind him. A thin-faced deputy, his mouth a
gaping trap for flies, was asleep on a dusty cot along
one wall.

The sheriff glanced up as Longarm pushed open the door and advanced on his desk.

"Sheriff Bond?"

"That's me."

Longarm introduced himself and showed the man his badge, after which he pulled a hard-backed chair over beside the sheriff's desk and sat down.

"What can I do for you, deputy?" Bond asked.

The sheriff was a lean, cleanly dressed man with knife-edged features, dark hair, and cold blue eyes. He looked honest—and Longarm was counting on this. "I'm looking for Clint Bolen. He's supposed to have a ranch around here."

"He did have a ranch around here."

"What do you mean?"

"He lit out—took his stock and vanished, but not without hiring a pretty good foreman. Petey Martin."

"Got any idea where he went?"

"West or north. Then again he could have headed into Montana. No one knows for sure."

"You mean he just left the ranch—abandoned it?"

"No, he sold it—for a good price, I hear."

"To whom?"

"Five brothers. Watts is their name. Tough, capable ranchers, from the looks of them—and not liable to take any guff from the Circle R or any of Roebuck's boys."

"Strange, isn't it? I mean, Bolen selling out like that."

"He must've had his reasons."

"I'd be glad to hear what you think some of them might be."

"My mother didn't bring her boy up to make fool

guesses. But maybe Bolen didn't like his spread surrounded by Roebuck land. Or maybe he pulled a fast one on J. T. and decided to light out."

"Has anyone been lookin' for him?"

"You're the first one. What's he done?"

"It's what him and Tate Rawson did."

Bond's face went cold at mention of Tate Rawson. It was obvious he didn't like the man. "Well, what did they do?"

"There's a good chance they killed a U.S. deputy marshal."

"Nothing on the wire about it."

"There wouldn't be. I'm handling it."

"Hard to believe Clint Bolen would be mixed up with Tate Rawson in something like that. I kind of liked him—his wife too. They got married here. She's a real nice looker."

"The way I figure it, Sheriff, he got mixed up with Tate because he didn't have much choice. But he's involved, sure enough. You seen Tate Rawson around here?"

"Nope. Not lately. And I hope I never do."

"You're right. He's a mean one. I'd appreciate it if you'd keep an eye out. I'm stayin' at the Cosmopolitan."

"Anything I can do to help."

"Thanks, Sheriff." Longarm stood up and shook Bond's hand. The handshake was solid. "With a man like Tate Rawson, I'd like to have someone at my back."

"You can count on me, Long."

Longarm glanced at the snoring deputy. Bond

grinned. "Don't mind Luke. He was awake all night chasin' drunks."

"Much obliged, Sheriff."

Leaving the sheriff's office, Longarm headed back to the hotel, intent on getting into a hot tub first and then packing it in. He had been in the saddle for three straight days, and his thigh wound was protesting mildly this unreasonable exertion.

The next morning, feeling a whole hell of a lot better, Longarm checked out of his hotel and, following directions given to him by the sheriff, rode out to the spread Clint Bolen had sold to the Watts brothers. When he reached the rangeland described to him, he found himself impressed by its lush, well-watered meadows and the fat, heavily larded look of the cattle the Watts clan had set loose upon it.

Riding up to the spread's ranch house close to noon, Longarm saw two of the Watts brothers stepping off the verandah of the main house to meet him. The house was a big one, and in pretty good repair. The brothers were not leaving anything to chance, however. A portion of the roof was under repair, and Longarm could see where they had just finished pointing up the fieldstone chimney.

The two men approaching Longarm were a formidable pair. There was not an ounce of tallow on their frames. They were powerful about the shoulders, with great hands and thick curls of nearly jet-black hair spilling down from under their wide, floppy-brimmed hats. Their clean-shaven faces were dark from the stubble that had sprung up since morning. As they walked toward Longarm, they peered out at him from under solid, slablike brows. At the moment their eyes were wary, if not downright unfriendly.

Pulling his horse to a halt a few feet from them, Longarm smiled and leaned casually forward onto his saddlehorn. "Howdy, gents," he said.

"Howdy," the nearest brother replied. "You another one of Circle R's crew?"

"Not likely," Longarm told him. "I'm lookin' for my sister, Melissa. I heard she married a friend of mine. Clint Bolen."

"A friend of yours, was he?"

"He was, and I hope he still is."

"That sister of yours is a pretty one. You don't look much like her, and that's a fact."

"Different mothers," he said. "And you're right. Melissa's beautiful. I'm sure happy for her. Clint's a fine man."

"You feel that way, do you?"

"Sure," Longarm said, gathering up his reins. "Why shouldn't I?"

"How come you're lookin' for him?"

"He wrote me a letter. Told me I could have a job here if I wanted. He said he'd be needin' good hands to run his spread."

"Ain't you heard?"

"That he sold out? Sure, I heard. The sheriff in town told me."

"So what're you doin' out here?"

"I want to know why he sold out and where he went—and where my sister might be."

For the first time the other one spoke up. "What's your name, mister?"

"Barstow. Neil Barstow."

93

"Light and rest a spell."

"Thanks."

Longarm dismounted and, leading his horse behind him, followed the two brothers to the house. He dropped the reins over the hitchrail in front of the verandah and climbed the stairs, following after them into the big house. The living room was spacious and cool, but it seemed dusty and seldom used. The kitchen was clean enough and looked well lived in.

As they slumped down around the kitchen table, a third Watts brother entered and put on some coffee. The two men Longarm had met outside introduced themselves as Tim and Josh. The fellow who just entered the kitchen was Dudley. So similar in build and look were the three brothers Longarm had difficulty telling them apart. After Dudley poured the coffee, he joined his brothers at the table and fixed his flaming blue eyes on Longarm.

"Lookin' for Clint, are you?"

Longarm nodded.

"You don't look like the sonofabitch Clint told me about. A feller name of Tate Rawson."

"Who's Tate Rawson?"

"A gunslinger who might be after Clint. If he shows up, we'll take care of him."

"Or anyone else from Roebuck's spread who comes here to give us any trouble," added Tim. "So far, we ain't had any trouble from this Roebuck feller. But I heard his foreman ain't so happy we made this deal with Bolen."

"Well, what happened? Why'd Clint sell out so fast?"

"The way I see it," Dudley drawled, "his past was

94

catching up to him. He needed to burn some bridges."

"That sure don't sound like Clint."

"I'm only tellin' you what I know. I didn't pry."

"Did Clint tell you where he was going?"

"West. To Oregon."

"Anyplace special in Oregon?"

"Nope."

"Damn. That's big country."

"Well, look for a place with lots of grass. He had five hundred cattle when he left here."

"Was Melissa all right? That'd be quite a trip for her."

Dudley shrugged. "Didn't see much of her."

"We did," said Tim, indicating himself and Josh. "She drove a wagon over our south range on her way into the mountains ahead of the herd. Me and Josh got a good look at her. She looked fine."

"Red hair?"

"That's her, all right."

Longarm nodded, as if mightily relieved, then finished his coffee and stood up. "Much obliged for the coffee, gents. I hope you like it here. Looks like a real nice spread. Too bad Clint had to sell it."

"Too bad for him," said Dudley, "but great for us."

The three brothers escorted Longarm from the house and stood back silently when he mounted up and rode out. Longarm could feel their eyes on his back when he rode through the gate, then turned west toward the mountains.

Oregon, Dudley said. So that was where Clint and Melissa had gone. As Longarm had remarked to

Dudley, Oregon was a big slice of country. Maybe he would get lucky and pick up their trail. You couldn't drive five hundred head of cattle and not leave some trace.

At least Longarm didn't think so.

Watching from a bluff behind the main ranch house, Tate waited patiently for the deputy to get well clear of the ranch buildings, his Winchester resting on a boulder in front of him. He glanced skyward. The sun was low in the sky, its rays giving him some trouble, spoiling his aim. He swore softly and pulled his hatbrim down farther to shade his eyes, then sighted along the rifle, his finger stealing in through the trigger guard. In a moment he was caressing the trigger, waiting for the deputy's back to clear a tangle of branches screening him as horse and rider swung west toward the mountains.

But he never got the chance to squeeze the trigger.

Something hit him with numbing force on the side of his head—just as a powerful hand snatched the rifle from his grasp. Tate started to turn, but another blow caught the back of his neck. He felt himself sagging to his knees, while the world spun sickeningly. Before he could rest on his knees, a heavy boot came out of nowhere and buried itself deep in Tate's stomach, sending him crashing back into the boulder. Tears blurring his vision, he sank down and began rolling on the ground, retching dryly, fruitlessly.

Two men of enormous size were bending over him, their dark, impassive faces watching with an intense lack of concern—as if they had just shot off the head of a rattler and were now watching its headless tail thrash about. Their faces hung in a red haze above him, and he could hear them calmly discussing him.

"He's the one Dudley told us about," said one.

The other nodded. "Yep. Ain't no question about that."

"What'll we do? Can't let him loose. A rattler like him. He woulda killed that rider for sure—and one of us'd be next."

The other nodded sagely. "I say we kill him."

"Maybe. But we oughta put it to a vote. Dudley can get awful riled if we go ahead on something like this without givin' him a chance to vote on it. You know what he was like after we stomped that sheepherder."

The other nodded. "Get this bastard's horse."

Tate's stomach had settled down some by this time and his eyes had cleared. But his neck was on fire where he'd been punched, and his gut ached something awful. Before he could utter any kind of a protest, they hauled him up onto his feet, then flung him over his horse's back. He sucked air into his lungs painfully and looked desperately, wildly about him.

One of the two men leaned close to him. "How you feelin', Mr. Tate?"

Tate snarled, "Let me go, you bastard. Soon's J. T. Roebuck hears about this, he'll run you off this land. You ain't got no right to be here!"

The big man's face darkened like a storm cloud. He brought his sixgun around in a wide, sweeping arc, and the last thing Tate remembered was the right side of his face exploding.

Tate could not believe the pain. It was like some incredible practical joke. Soon, whatever it was would let up. He would feel immediate relief and everyone would have a good laugh.

Lying flat on his back on a cot, Tate waited. But there was no relief from the awful pain. In fact, as he grew more alert to his surroundings—a small grain room with a single window just above his head—the pain grew even more intense. He started to move his jaw involuntarily to swallow the saliva clogging his mouth. Instantly a sudden, terrible bolt of pain shot up through the back of his jaw into his right eye-socket, like a fist.

Only gradually did the awesome shock of pain subside. He lay panting, his jaw held rigid, gradually becoming aware that he was seeing clearly only out of the left side of his face. With extreme care he lifted his hand to his right eye and to his horror found nothing there but a scabbed lid sunk into an empty socket. His trembling fingers felt beneath the eye-socket and found a jagged, open wound as wide as two fingers. The wound ran down his face from the temple all the way to his mouth. Any pressure at all on his right cheekbone brought an immediate surge of pain.

He let his hand drop and slowly, gingerly, raised himself onto one elbow, then eased himself upright to a sitting position. Leaning back against the wall, he stared miserably through his remaining eye at the chair sitting against the wall opposite him. The bright light of morning knifed in through the window. It was the intensity of this sunlight that had awakened him. He heard movement in the next room. Heavy feet caused the wall to tremble slightly against his back. Booming voices reverberated as the men conversed casually. He could not catch individual words often, and when he did, little of what he heard made sense.

Occasionally there were sudden, savage outbursts of laughter—and this infuriated Tate. That he could be in this condition, suffering like this, while they who had caused it went about their business as usual, laughing and making jests, was almost more than he could bear. There was absolutely no retribution too extreme, no form of torture too refined that he would not gladly visit upon these men. Tate did not believe in God. As a result he could not pray to Him to deliver these men to him for vengeance.

But he did pray—constantly, fervently—to another, darker power, one he only dimly sensed.

The door swung open and one of the men stood in the doorway, his huge frame filling it.

"He's awake, all right," he called back over his shoulders. "He's sittin' up!"

"Bring him in here then," a heavy, powerful voice directed.

The giant strode into the room and took Tate by his shirt collar and dragged him out of the room and into the kitchen. As he was unable to hold his head steady, each movement caused sharp, bludgeoning bursts of pain to rocket through Tate's skull. By the time he was dropped to the kitchen floor, he was groaning softly, unashamedly.

Four men were sitting around the kitchen table, watching. The fifth one left Tate and sat down beside them, pulling a mug of coffee closer. All five men looked down at him with a curious, reflective detachment.

One of the men said, "Clint Bolen told me about you, Tate. He said you might be after him. You're Roebuck's hired gun, ain't you?"

It was impossible for Tate to reply, even if he had a mind to. He stared bleakly up at the five men without making any effort to respond.

Another of the men leaned forward, peering intently down at Tate. "Answer Dudley, mister! You workin' for Roebuck?"

Again Tate made no attempt to reply. The slightest movement of his jaw would send terrible daggers of pain deep into his skull. The jaw was broken, shattered by the force of that sixgun's barrel. The fellow who had asked the question—Dudley—took this as simple defiance. He got up swiftly and kicked Tate in the ribs. Tate felt one of them snap as he went tumbling like a bedroll across the floor. The wall stopped him with numbing force.

He could not move and lay with his back to the five brothers, his face flat against the wall, the pain surging through him like a tide. He felt a rough hand on his shoulder and was pulled back and around. One of the brothers—this fellow had a gray streak running through his thick, black hair—peered at him closely.

"Hell, Matthew. What'd you hit him with yesterday? Looks like his jaw might be broken."

"Just my gunbarrel, Josh."

"You sure it's broken?" Dudley asked.

Josh took Tate's chin in his hand and moved it from side to side. Tate screeched in agony as the sound of grating bone filled the kitchen. Josh nodded in satisfaction and let go of Tate's chin.

"It's broken, all right," Josh said, peering more closely at the bloodied eyesocket. "And it looks like you done poked out his eye, too, Matt."

Matthew shrugged. "I know that. He lost it when I flung him over his horse. I told Paul to go back after it, but he couldn't find it."

"I didn't look very long," Paul admitted.

Josh stood up and stared reflectively down at Tate. "Hell, we ain't goin' to get much out of a man with a broken jaw. I say we finish him. What do you say, Dudley?"

"There ain't no question in my mind," Dudley responded. "He's the one Clint warned me about—the hired killer who works for Roebuck."

"I say kill the sonofabitch," said Matthew. "He was fixin' to blow that Barstow feller clear out of his saddle."

"And you can bet your ass we would've been next," commented Josh grimly.

"I say kill him," Matthew repeated.

"Not so fast," said Paul. "Let's do this right. Put it to a vote."

"That's right," said Dudley. "I say we vote."

"Sure," said Matthew. "I don't mind. All them as

wants to kill this no-account backshootin' skunk, raise your hands."

Matthew and Dudley raised their hands. Paul and the other two did not. Tate could hardly believe it. *They were not going to kill him!*

"All right," said Dudley. "We won't kill him— not outright, that is. But I say we send him the hell out of here. How's that sound?"

"Suits me," said Paul, nodding eagerly.

Josh and the youngest one agreed.

Matthew thought a moment, then grinned. "Say, boys, we still got that outlaw bronc, ain't we?"

"That's right," Dudley said. "He's still out there, raising hell. And I'm beginning to think he's too mean to service them dams we got in Montana."

"That's the way it looks to me. So I say we get rid of them both. Tie this sonofabitch to the bronc's back, and send them both into the mountains. That way, we'll get rid of two outlaws at the same time."

There was no further discussion. The matter was settled.

When Dudley reached the stable door, he released Tate and dumped him on the ground, then went inside with Matthew. Caught in a dazed web of pain, Tate watched as the two men led the mustang out of the barn. It was a small paint with wild eyes and nervous feet. Its nostrils flared repeatedly, and it began to snort as the brothers crowded around. Paul held a hat over the animal's eyes, while Tim hung on to the hackamore.

Tate felt himself being lifted, then flung down onto the bronc's back. They weren't bothering with a saddle, just what felt like an old saddle blanket. Tate was thrust forward onto the horse's neck. Freshly moistened strips of rawhide were wrapped around his wrists and ankles, then the wrists were drawn together under the bronc's neck, while his ankles were pulled tightly under the bronc's belly.

Tate tried to keep his left cheek down, snug against the bronc's mane to protect his shattered cheekbone, but the horse was already bucking excitedly, making this impossible. Out of the corner of his eye, he saw Matthew and Dudley mounting their own horses.

One brother lifted his hat. The other stepped away from the bronc, releasing the hackamore. At the same time Matthew and Dudley let out a series of piercing yips and waved their hats in the air. The bronc bucked once, twice—then, as the two riders charged it, the crazed animal bolted past them and across the compound out through the gate, the two mounted brothers pursuing it gleefully.

Drawing their sidearms, they began firing over the head of the already maddened bronc, turning it toward the mountains. For close to an hour the two riders, shooting and yelling, drove the horse before them, thoroughly demoralizing the animal as it tried to outrun its pursuers and shake from its back the unconscious burden fastened to it. By this time the bronc was close to exhaustion as it scrambled higher into the rocks ahead of them, its neck flecked with foam.

The two men pulled up, smiling broadly. "That's far enough, I reckon," Dudley told Matthew.

"That poor sonofabitch won't get peeled off that bronc until next spring," Matthew agreed.

"All we got to do now is wait for Roebuck to come askin' after him."

"Or his foreman."

"Yeah," Dudley said, grinning broadly. "I can't wait."

Chapter Seven

Bim Holley stirred suddenly and sat up on his cot. His heart was pounding. He thought he had heard something outside the cabin. He sat awhile on the cot, listening.

But all he heard was the clear chattering of the birds, their calls a delightful music echoing in the canyon. Bim took a deep breath. He was feeling poorly this morning, his head thick with muddle— but them birds was feelin' just fine. He pulled on his boots and stood up.

A man well past sixty, Bim's thinning hair and beard were snow white, except for that portion of his beard stained mahogany from the chewing tobacco constantly dribbling from the corner of his mouth. He was wearing a faded red woolen undershirt. Finished dressing, he tucked the tops of his worn Levi's into his boots. The leather about the boots' ankles was worn as thin as cigarette paper and the soles offered little protection from the rocky ground outside his cabin. For months now he had been meaning to ride into Pine Ridge to get himself a new pair. But he just didn't feel up to the trip, especially now that his pack mule had died on him.

His heart was still pounding. Why, he had no idea. The altitude, maybe. He looked over at the cold woodstove. He had been too tired to bring in fresh kindling the night before. Now he would have to go out into the damp, gray, dewladen morning and search for what he could never find this early—dry wood. He shook his head at the misery of it and decided on a breakfast of cold pemmican.

He moved gingerly over to the corner where he stored his provisions, opened a rawhide sack, and pulled out a strip of dessicated venison. He had solidified the cured meat with hot marrow fat, and was soon chomping on the rich fare with his remaining teeth. He licked his fingers when he had finished his meal, feeling much better.

Hell's fire, he told himself, a man didn't always need a hot breakfast.

Still, he would like a fire in the stove. He opened the cabin door and stepped out. There might be some dry wood behind the shed out back. Besides, he couldn't stay in the cabin any more. He had to pee.

He was standing beside the shed, buttoning up his fly, when he heard a horse stamp its feet. He walked on around the shed and saw a pony standing there, congealed lather hanging in long strings from its mouth. Someone was clinging to the pony. No.

Someone was tied to it. Carefully, Bim picked his way over the stony ground to the trembling pony. Its flanks were quivering almost continuously.

The rider was more under the paint than on it. Tight rawhide had been wrapped around his wrists and ankles. So deeply had they cut into the flesh, Bim could barely see the individual strands. From repeated brushings against rocks and bushes, the man's shirt and pants had been ripped from his torso. The bared skin was as raw as uncooked beefsteak. The crazed bronc, frantic to be rid of his rider, must have tried repeatedly to brush off the man tied to him by dragging him against rock walls, brush, and perhaps even trees.

Bim could not see the man's face. It was turned away from him, facing in under the bronc's body.

Bim leaned close to the battered piece of flesh and listened. Above the thudding of his own heart, he could still hear the man's shallow breathing. Amazed that after all this the man was still alive, Bim stepped back. The bronc's eyes were bloodshot but steady, looking upon him almost hopefully, as if the animal expected Bim to relieve it of its awful burden.

Bim hurried back to his cabin and returned with his knife. He cut the man free. The fellow slumped heavily to the ground. Bim attempted to lift the unconscious man onto his shoulders to carry him into the cabin. It was impossible. The exertion nearly caused his own collapse. He dragged the man across the ground and into his cabin. Once inside, puffing like a steam engine, Bim slumped down onto his cot to regain his breath. Then, with a grim sense of purpose, he got up and lugged the man over to his cot, dumping him unceremoniously down onto it.

Dizzy from the exertion, a cold sweat breaking out on his forehead, he looked down at the unconscious man. What he saw appalled him. The man's body was severely beaten. His clothes hung in bloody tatters from his frame. But it was the man's ravaged face that sickened him the most. Thick encrustings of congealed blood caked the man's nostrils. His lips were swollen enormously. The jawline was crooked, indicating that the jaw was broken as well, all the damage evidently stemming from a single terrible blow which had laid open the right half of his face, crushing the cheekbone and popping the eye, leaving only the black, scabbed socket. For a moment Bim had the queer notion he could see through that hole into the man's brain.

It was incredible the poor bastard was still alive.

Bim should get help for him, he realized. And yet he could not trust Polk or any of his crazy gang. The only reason they had left off beating up on him was because they were finally convinced he had nothing worth robbing—and that his mine was a dry hole. Which it was. Bim shrugged. He would simply have to take care of this poor sonofabitch himself.

First he'd clean him off and then do what he could to set that broken jaw. After that he'd fix him up with some pemmican stew—if he could figure a way to feed it to him. Grabbing a bucket, Bim hurried from the cabin to get water from the stream, the awful plight of a fellow human being arousing him as nothing else had during these last miserable, lonely years.

Longarm reined in his dun, folded his arm over the pommel, and peered over the lip of the canyon at the miner's shack below him. There was a small shed alongside it, and the mouth of a played-out mine showing about fifty yards further down. A thin trace of wood smoke lifted from the shack's chimney. It was the powerful scent of woodsmoke that had drawn him to this canyon—reminding him of just how long it had been since he had last slept under a roof or eaten with his elbows on a table.

At first it had been a simple matter to track Clint Bolen's herd. The rutted trail left by the wagon Clint had purchased in Pine Ridge had been especially helpful. But once into the mountains, Longarm had been overtaken by a pounding three-day rain that had wiped out all tracks. One pass took him clear to Oregon, and he had ridden through it in search of Bolen and his herd. But in town after town, he found no sign whatever of Clint Bolen and his lovely wife, let alone that herd of five hundred cattle. Now, back in the Salmon River Mountains, he was backtracking, looking for another pass.

It was near the end of a long, hard day's ride. As he sat his horse, the smell of the woodsmoke grew more seductive with each passing moment. This miner's shack was the only sign of human habitation he had come on in three days. Nudging his horse back from the lip of the canyon, he turned it and followed a game trail toward canyon's floor, letting the dun choose its own pace as it picked its way along the precarious trail. When finally he reached the bottom, he was some distance from the miner's shack. Dusk was falling by the time he had doubled back to it.

"Hello, the cabin!" he called.

The door opened. A white-haired oldtimer appeared in the doorway. He did not look well, and was holding onto the doorframe with one hand as he peered out through the gathering darkness at Longarm.

"Howdy," said Longarm from the saddle. He made no effort to dismount. "That woodsmoke fetched me. Thought there might be a fire and a pot of coffee under it."

"Why, sure, stranger," the miner said, cheerfully enough. "Light and set awhile. Spend the night if you've a mind. Glad for the company."

"I'll just take care of my horse first," Longarm told him, dismounting.

"There's oats in the shed over there and a water bucket. The stream's yonder."

Longarm caught sight of the stream and nodded. "Thanks," he said, and led his horse toward the shed.

The first thing Longarm noticed when he entered was the man lying on a hay mattress beside the stove. He was the miner's partner, Longarm figured. Judging from his appearance, he must have suffered some fearful accident. Torn strips from a wool shirt had been wound tightly around his face and head so that the only part of his face that was clearly visible was his left eye.

Longarm put down his gear in the corner and walked over to the table where the miner was placing down a pot of coffee. The injured man raised his head and regarded Longarm closely with his one eye. He seemed alert enough, but he appeared to be having trouble focusing his remaining eye. Longarm nodded to him. The fellow let himself rest back on the mattress, his one eye still fastened on Longarm.

The miner sat down at the table across from Longarm, poured both of them a cup of coffee, then pushed a cup at Longarm. Longarm took the steaming black liquid gratefully.

"Much obliged," he said.

"No trouble. I always keep a pot on," the miner said.

"Name's Long," Longarm said, sipping the coffee. "Custis Long."

"They calls me Bim. I almost forget what my last name was. I don't use it none, and it don't mean nothing to anyone anymore—not that it ever did. What're you doin' scratchin' around in these parts?"

"I'm looking for someone—someone pushing a herd through these mountains to Oregon. I'd like to catch up to them."

"Relatives?"

"Nope."

"You a lawman?"

"Deputy U.S. marshal."

"Well, I don't hold that against you. A man's got to do something to live."

"You got it right, oldtimer."

"Well, you're still welcome to bunk here for the night."

"I appreciate that." Longarm glanced at the man's injured partner. "What happened to your partner?"

111

"He ain't my partner. He just happened by not long ago."

"He looks pretty torn up."

"He is that. Got a broken jaw, a shattered cheekbone, some busted ribs. And he lost an eye somewhere between here and there."

"How'd he get here?"

"Someone tied him to a wild bronc. The bronc's gone—like wind in the springtime."

"How do you feed him?"

The old man smiled proudly. "I been fixin' him pemmican soup, and feedin' it to him through a hollow reed. I found the reeds down along the stream. They make dandy straws."

"What's his name?"

The miner shrugged. "He ain't said a word to me since he got here. A man can't get much past a busted jaw, and I got that bandage pretty tight—as tight as I could manage it."

Longarm nodded. It might have seemed a foolish question to the miner, but the fellow might have had some identification on him, or maybe they could have communicated by writing notes to each other. Evidently that possibility had not occurred to either man.

"You set his jaw?"

"As best I could."

Longarm looked more closely at the injured man. The poor sonofabitch was watching them both closely, and for a fleeting second Longarm found something oddly familiar about the man. But he realized at once the impossibility of this.

Longarm looked back at the old miner. He was

out of his chair now, building what supper he could for them, given the limitations of his cupboard. Before long, the small cabin was alive with the sound of sizzling venison as it danced in the skillet beside slices of potatoes and what looked like squirrel corn. The bacon fat was abundant, and in a well-greased Dutch oven beside the skillet sourdough biscuits were in the making.

Under the conditions, the meal, topped off with fresh hot coffee, was a masterpiece. With a pleased Bim chuckling, Longarm used a portion of his sourdough biscuit to clean off his plate. Shaking his head in appreciation at Bim's culinary skills, Longarm popped the last of the biscuit into his mouth.

"Much obliged, Bim," Longarm told him. "Don't know when a meal ever went down better."

"Nice to have a fellow human to cook for," Bim acknowledged, his face glowing with pleasure at the compliment.

Longarm cleaned up the dishes and cooking utensils while the miner fed the injured man his bowl of pemmican soup. By the time he and Longarm were ready to turn in, the old miner didn't look so good. His face was pale and beads of cold sweat stood out on his forehead.

"You all right?" Longarm asked him.

"A touch of indigestion, might be," Bim said, clenching his fist and rapping his solar plexus lightly. "I shouldn't ought to enjoy myself that much when I eat. I allus pay for it, seems like."

Sitting wearily down onto his cot, he took out a filthy handkerchief and mopped the perspiration pouring off his face.

"Want some water to settle your stomach?"

"There's a bottle of whiskey in the cabinet over the headboard. I'd be obliged if you'd get it for me."

"I'll get it. Stay right there."

As Bim sucked on the whiskey bottle, his color returned and he grinned up at Longarm in some relief. "That's all I needed," he said, stoppering the bottle and handing it back to Longarm. "Help yourself."

Longarm took a healthy belt and returned the bottle to the cupboard. With a deep, weary sigh the miner kicked off his boots and hoisted his feet up onto the cot. Pulling a ragged buffalo robe about his shoulders, he rolled over to face the wall. In a moment Longarm heard the man's steady breathing and knew he was asleep. He glanced over at the injured man huddled on the straw mattress. His single eye was shut also; he too was apparently asleep.

Longarm went over to his pile of gear in the corner, opened up his sleeping bag, and bedded down on the dirt floor. His belly full, his soul for the moment content, he fell asleep almost instantly.

He awoke with the sound of birds chirping merrily. Longarm liked the way their song echoed in the canyon. He sat up, alert at once, for he saw that the injured man was already awake, sitting up on his straw mattress. With his one baleful eye he was regarding Longarm closely.

Longarm nodded to him, reached for his hat, and got to his feet. He had a notion to take off his clothes and take a dip in the stream below the cabin. He saw no reason for disturbing the old miner if he didn't have to do so.

Then he glanced more closely at Bim. He was dead to the world, his face still turned to the wall. And in that instant Longarm knew the old man *was* dead.

He hurried over and laid a hand on his shoulder. The body under the blanket was heavy, unyielding, cold to his touch. The old man's entire bulk seemed to have shrunk in on itself, as if something vital had been withdrawn. Longarm turned him over and looked down into the dead, slack face, the eyes still closed, a thin, barely perceptible smile on his face.

The lucky sonofabitch, Longarm said to himself wonderingly. He had died peacefully in his sleep.

When Longarm returned to the cabin later that morning after burying Bim, he found himself musing on the odd chance that had brought him to this shack for that one last dinner with the old man. The injured man, his head and face still heavily swathed in bandages, had helped Longarm carry out the dead miner and had helped dig the grave. Then he had stood watching the burial from a slight distance, as if such displays of emotion were foreign to him. Then he had returned to the cabin ahead of Longarm and was now back on his straw mattress, watching Longarm alertly out of his one eye.

Longarm slacked wearily down at the table.

"Dammit," he said to the man. "What's your name, mister?"

The man's eye narrowed and Longarm realized the man was smiling. He pointed to Longarm, then to himself. *You name me* was the gesture's unmistakable meaning.

"All right," Longarm told him. "You only got one eye left. So I'm calling you Cyclops. He was a big Greek fellow with only one eye in the center of his forehead. I'll call you Cy for short."

The man nodded in acceptance.

"You can stay here if you want," Longarm told him. "Or you can move out with me. I'm looking for a gent and his wife who're driving a herd to Oregon. I figure they've already got there by now, but I'm going to catch up to them, come hell or high water. I can make you my unofficial deputy until that jaw of yours heals. How's that sound?"

The man Longarm had just christened Cy got to his feet with surprising alacrity and stood ready—almost eager, it seemed—to pull out with Longarm. Longarm was pleased, if not a little annoyed, at how spry Cy now appeared to be. While Bim was alive, Cy had sat back without lifting a hand and let the old man wait on him hand and foot.

The two men had ridden at least ten miles further into the canyon, following the stream that dribbled past the entrance to Bim's mine. Longarm had a hunch. It seemed to him that if there was another way through these mountains, this stream might well point the way.

Longarm glanced at Cy, who was riding abreast of him. He was astride the miner's fat old gelding. Cy's face was still bandaged heavily, and Longarm could not help but notice how comically the clothes Cy had taken from Bim's trunk billowed on the man's spare frame. Cy had also taken Bim's buffalo robe. Fastened about his neck with a huge safety pin, it flowed out behind him like an opera cloak. But it was the old miner's wide-brimmed hat, worn with the brim pulled down over his face and neck, that gave to the one-eyed man's macabre appearance its final, desperate touch.

Longarm could not help wondering what had really happened to Cy. There was a grimness about him, accentuated by his complete silence, that impressed Longarm. The man did not ask for quarter, nor did he complain of his terrible condition. He accepted it almost casually and rode on implacably, a remarkable apparition. Despite every attempt on Longarm's part to shake it, Cy gave him a troubling, unshakable sense of unease.

Longarm clattered over a stretch of caprock and rounded a sharp bend in the canyon. He pulled up in disappointment.

Just ahead of him loomed a sheer wall of rock, solid and unbroken, save for a single narrow defile through which the stream they had been following issued. Longarm swore bitterly as he splashed through a shallow pond in front of the rock face. When he reached the wall, he leaned his head against it and heard the sound of the freshet plunging toward him through the rock.

Longarm shook his head in frustration. On his way to that promised land in Oregon, Bolen could not have taken his herd through here. Then Longarm saw a narrow, shale-littered game trail leading to the canyon rim high above.

"Stay here, Cy," he said. "I'm going up there, see what's beyond this rock wall."

Cy nodded slightly, leaning forward to pat his horse's neck.

Longarm rode as high as he could on the trail, then dismounted three-quarters of the way up to lead his horse the rest of the way to the rim. Once on solid ground, he left the canyon behind and rode further west toward a timbered plateau to get a better glimpse of what lay ahead. As his eye gazed out over the snowcapped peaks and towering crags, he saw no pass, no easy way through the towering escarpment.

The sound of hoofs came to him dimly from the canyon behind him. He turned his mount and rode back to the rim and looked down. He was in time to see Cy riding off in the company of four riders. The men weren't cowhands, from the look of their well-oiled, strapped-down sidearms. Outlaws, more than likely, holed up in these impenetrable mountains.

And now they had Cy. What the hell did they want him for? Longarm swore. The old miner had felt a responsibility for that poor, ruined sonofabitch. And so did Longarm.

Keeping to the canyon's rim, Longarm followed the five riders. After a quarter of a mile, they turned down a side canyon, then rode into a narrow cleft barely able to admit them, except in single file. From high above, Longarm watched as they vanished into it. The passageway evidently led to another canyon or trail leading through these mountains—or, more likely, to the gang's hideout.

If Longarm were to go after them, he would have to regain the canyon floor. Without hesitation, he turned his mount and headed back to the game trail that would take him back down.

Chapter Eight

It was late that same afternoon when Longarm rode cautiously through the narrow defile and emerged onto the broad valley he found on the other side. Gently undulating pastures, chin high with lush grasses, extended as far as the eye could see. At Longarm's back great walls of rock towered skyward, shutting out the world he had left behind. And miles ahead of him, barely visible in the distance, Longarm saw a narrow pass leading into the valley from the west.

It occurred to him that once having passed through the more northerly pass into Oregon, Clint could have doubled back through that pass into this nearly inaccessible valley, a perfect place for him to settle, providing he had five hundred head of cattle and money enough to build. And Clint Bolen had both in abundance.

Keeping in the cool shadows beneath the cliff walls, Longarm rode into the valley, descending into deep swells so lush the grass brushed the belly of his dun. Rabbits bounded off soundlessly through the thick grass. Passing a shoulder of rock, he caught sight of three buildings far across the flat on the other side of valley—a house, a bunkhouse, and a barn. He could barely make out the corrals and the horses grazing behind the barn. But he couldn't miss the beef cattle that dotted the valley floor and the broad, grassy mountain slopes. Just about five hundred head of cattle, he figured.

Maybe—just maybe—he had found Clint Bolen.

But what did those four gunslicks have to do with Clint and Melissa Bolen?

Keeping to the swales, Longarm headed across the valley toward the ranch houses. When he got closer, he caught sight of a broad stream that cut across the flat in front of the ranch. Anyone approaching those buildings would have to cross the open flat in front of it, then ford the stream—all in full view of the ranch's occupants.

He turned his horse and, instead of heading directly for the ranch, rode toward the timbered mountain flanks behind it. Reaching the timber, Longarm kept within it as he circled the valley. It was night when he rode out of the timber to look down upon the ranch buildings. The rising moon was whitening the sky beyond the mountains, but it was not visible yet. Longarm dismounted, tethered his dun, then darted down the slope to the bunkhouse and checked it out. Peering in through the dirt-encrusted windows, he could not make out a single made-up bunk or cot. It was empty.

He glanced at the small ranch house. Oil lamps inside the small frame building illuminated the rooms. The light coming from two front windows cast bright, rectangular patches on the front yard. As he watched, a shadow moved across one of the front windows and a moment later the door swung open, flooding light down the wooden steps. A man stepped to the edge of the porch and emptied a slop-jar.

As soon as the man went back inside, Longarm darted to the rear of the house, flattened himself against the wall, and listened. He heard the lazy hum of voices inside. Laughter. Harsh, masculine. He moved along the wall and peered into the room from which most of the sound was coming. The four men he had seen earlier with Cy were at a small table, playing poker.

And then he saw Cy.

Only it wasn't Cy. It was Tate Rawson!

The bandage that had covered his face was gone. He had shaved off his beard, revealing a livid scar that ran from his sunken cheekbone to the corner of his mouth. A leather patch covered his empty eye-socket. At the moment Tate was leaning against a wall, watching the four men at the table, a Colt .45 stuck in his belt. From someone he had gotten a pair of Levi's that fit, and a red checked shirt. He looked reasonably fit now—and every inch the killer he was.

Longarm recalled his earlier misgivings—slight

though they were—about the injured man on the straw mattress. Bitterly, he berated himself. Even though he had caught only one fleeting glimpse of Tate in Roebuck's office, it should have been sufficient.

Longarm moved further along the wall and came to another window that opened onto the bedroom. Peering through it, he saw Melissa on the bed, naked, her hands tied to the bedposts behind her head, her ankles tied to those at her feet. Her head was twisted to one side, her cheek swollen where she had been struck repeatedly. She was crying softly, her sobs coming faintly to him through the window. Another member of the gang was standing before the closed door, buckling on his pants and preparing to go back out and rejoin the others.

On the floor between the bed and the window, Longarm glimpsed a slumped body. On tiptoes, he peered closer. It was Clint Bolen. The man was unconscious. His face had been beaten almost to a pulp. His eyes were swollen shut and his nose was simply a bloody blister over a torn, gaping hole that had been his mouth.

Longarm took a deep breath and backed away.

He could only guess what must have happened. Evidently Clint had driven his herd into this valley through that pass, thinking this land and these buildings were his for the taking—perhaps he had paid for them at some land office—and what he had found here were these outlaws. They had accepted the gift of all these beef cattle, obviously, and had taken anything else of value Clint Bolen had, including his wife.

Longarm needed a diversion.

He cut back behind the bunkhouse, then entered the barn. Reaching for a lantern, he almost sprawled headlong over a body dumped in a corner. Longarm examined it. A bullet had taken the dead man in the heart. He had been dead for some time, the smell of putrefaction hanging heavy about him. This must be the foreman Bolen had hired and whose hoofprints Longarm had noticed along with Bolen's as he tracked the herd.

After Longarm took down the lantern, he let out what horses remained in their stalls, lit the lantern, then tossed it up into the hayloft, making sure the chimney shattered against a beam. The flames caught the hay instantly. Longarm ran back to the rear of the house and waited. The men were so intent on their card game that not until the barn's roof was half devoured, with sparks shooting high into the sky, did anyone inside the ranch house notice.

"Goddamn it!" one of the men cried, flinging open the door. "Who started that?"

"It sure as hell wasn't no dead man," another said, getting up from his chair so quickly he knocked it to the floor.

"It's that deputy!" Tate Rawson cried, following the first one out the door. "I told you guys to post a guard!"

As the living room emptied, Longarm lifted the bedroom window sash and climbed inside. Stepping over Clint Bolen's body, he hurried to the door and opened it a crack to make sure the others were all gone. Satisfied, he went back to the bed and cut Melissa Bolen loose.

"Who are you?" she cried through torn lips, her words barely distinguishable.

"Name's Long. Custis Long. I'm a deputy U.S. marshal. Help me get your husband out of here—that's who it is, isn't it?"

"Yes."

As Melissa picked up her clothes, which were scattered all over the floor, Longarm peered down at the man he had last seen aiming a sixgun at him through the rain. That Bolen had not succeeded in killing him had been pure chance. Even so, Longarm doubted if he would have wished this terrible retribution on him—or any man.

As soon as Melissa was dressed, he took Bolen under his armpits and lifted him up onto the windowsill. Melissa took his feet and guided them out the window, while Longarm still held him about the waist.

"I'll lift him down to you," Longarm told her.

She scrambled out the window and as carefully as possible, Longarm lowered Bolen into her arms. Swiftly, she lowered him to the ground.

"Drag him over behind the bunkhouse," Longarm told her.

She grabbed her husband under the arms and soon disappeared into the night.

By this time night had been transformed into a garish, unnatural day as the flames devouring the barn filled the night with a hellish glow. Longarm could hear the men running about in the yard, doing what they could to quench the flames. Longarm placed both hands on the windowsill and was about to jump down when he heard heavy footsteps behind him. He drew back from the window and whirled. One of the gang members, his face black with rage, stormed into the bedroom, gun drawn.

Longarm crabbed sideways and reached across to draw his Colt. The weapon spat almost automatically as he drew it. Two slugs pounded into the astonished gang member's stomach. He buckled and fired a round into the floor. Behind him, the cabin door was flung wide and two more men rushed in, one of them bald as a doorknob. They both had drawn guns, and after one look at Longarm they began firing. Longarm ducked out of sight, snatched up an oil lamp, and flung it into the other room. Peering after it, he saw the lamp shatter on the floor in front of the two men. A sheet of flame swept across the floor and up the wall.

The two men ducked back hastily. In that movement they doomed themselves as the vaulting flames cut them off from the outside doorway. Longarm stepped into the room, grabbed another lamp, and added its fuel to the first. The two men turned on him, but Longarm's gun was out, bucking lethally. The bald fellow pitched forward into the flames. Longarm ducked back into the bedroom and flung himself out the open window, shattering the windowpanes and taking portions of the sash with him.

He landed heavily, rolled over, and, glancing back, saw a man struggling to reach the window. The fire was in the bedroom with him, its tongues licking the walls all around him. His clothes smoking, his hair on fire, the man staggered to the open window. Longarm lifted his .44, aimed carefully, and fired into the man's face. The round knocked him back into the roaring inferno.

The flames danced higher, slicing hungrily through the roof. Sparks and flaming embers showered down. The screams coming from within the cabin ceased. Longarm darted toward the barn and was just in time to see two men, one of them Tate Rawson, vanish into the night, lugging saddles they had rescued from the barn's tack room. Longarm went after them, but a sudden fusillade from behind the flaming barn reminded him that while Tate and the other one might be invisible to him, Longarm was in full view.

He broke back behind the bunkhouse. A moment or two later, Tate and the other man emerged from the night, lashing their horses. As they galloped past, Longarm ran out after them and began firing. But his shots were wasted. And in a moment Tate Rawson and the other one were gone.

Longarm returned to Melissa. She was sitting crosslegged in the grass, her husband's head resting in her lap.

"Did you see the one with Tate?"

"Yes."

"Who was he?"

"Henry Polk, the leader of the gang."

"Who the hell were these guys?"

"I heard them talking. They robbed stages in California before coming here about six months ago. The others with him were Welch, Connors, and a man they called Fitz. Fitz was the worst."

"Can you describe him?"

"He was bald."

"You can forget about him. He's fryin' back there in the house."

"Oh, my God," she breathed. "But . . . I don't care. He was . . . a monster."

"He the one beat up Clint?"

"They all beat up Clint," she said, her voice flat, her empty, desolate eyes fixed on her husband's slack face. "And me."

"But why didn't Tate help you? I thought him and Clint worked together."

"They did—until you took back the records. It was J. T. who sent Tate after us. Tate said something about getting paid a good amount by Roebuck if he brought back Clint's scalp—and yours." She shuddered at the thought. "He . . . attacked me as soon as he got here. And when Clint tried to stop him, Tate beat him even worse than the others. . . ."

She hung her head and compressed her lips grimly, too angry now for tears. He waited a decent interval before questioning her further.

"How'd it happen? You getting mixed up with them, I mean."

"They were here in the house when we rode up. They seemed friendly enough and Clint offered them jobs working for him. They seemed to like the idea —until they found Clint's saddlebags with the money. Then they turned on us—like wild beasts."

"When was this?"

"Two days ago. After that they got drunk and real wild and started talking about an old miner back in the mountains. Some of them insisted he had dug out a fortune. Others laughed. Some of them rode off to find out, leaving Fitz to guard me and Clint."

129

"And that's when Fitz went after you."

"That's when he finished what he and the others had started the night before," she explained wearily, her voice dead now, expressionless.

She was in no condition to talk any further. Longarm suggested they take refuge in the bunkhouse for the remainder of the night. They carried the still unconscious Bolen inside it, found a bed not too dusty for him, and let him down onto it. In a matter of minutes, curled up on a motheaten blanket beside her husband's cot, Melissa dropped off into an exhausted sleep.

Longarm dragged one of the cots outside, set it down beside the bunkhouse facing the still burning barn, then took out a cheroot to think things over. He had a pretty good idea what had happened when the four gang members came on Tate in the canyon. Rawson must have pulled away his bandages enough to tell the four riders how much he could do for them if they helped him—and J. T. Roebuck. Since he knew of the miner's death, he would most likely have apprised the men of this, then told them who he was looking for and why. When he realized who the gang was holding, Longarm could imagine the eagerness with which he returned with them.

And now Rawson was fleeing back to J. T. Roebuck with the gang leader, Polk. Well, there was no problem in that for Longarm. He would know where to find them both. The flames from the barn were dying rapidly. Longarm looked past the glowing beams and mounds of ash. The terrified horses he had released were bunched in the farthest corner of the corral. He got up from the cot and walked over to inspect the cabin's gutted, smoldering shell. The ruins were still alive with busy tongues of flame. He thought he could smell, however faintly, the sickly-sweet stench of roasted carcasses.

Somewhere, he knew, there was a dodger out on these men. But they wouldn't be needed now.

Longarm returned to his cot and slept.

It was dawn, a chilly dawn. Melissa was shaking Longarm anxiously. "Mr. Long! Please! Get up!"

Longarm sat up quickly. "What is it?"

"It's Clint!"

Longarm grabbed his hat and followed Melissa into the bunkhouse. Clint was conscious, but only barely. A thin trickle of blood streamed from a corner of his mouth. He did not look good. Longarm bent over him.

"They busted my ribs," he whispered to Longarm. "When I cough, I bring up blood. I'm hurt bad, deputy. I think I'm goin' to die."

"A few busted ribs won't kill you."

"It ain't only that," he whispered, his voice a painful rasp. "They kicked me in the head . . . too many times. I can't see no more, and I keep passin' out."

Longarm glanced unhappily at Melissa. Bolen's head injuries alone could be fatal, and if the broken ribs had torn up his lungs sufficiently, there was little chance he would leave this bunkhouse alive. From the sound of the man's labored, painful breathing, Longarm realized the man was bleeding internally. Judging from the deathly white cast to his face, he was losing blood fast.

131

Longarm leaned close to him. "Listen, Clint. You're going to be all right. We'll get you to a town and a doctor."

"I don't believe you, deputy. There's no town near enough for me. And no doctor who can help. I'm going to die."

Longarm made no more effort to deny the obvious. "All right, Clint," he said. "But before you go, why not do your wife a favor?"

"What do you mean?"

"Tell me, with Melissa as a witness, who killed Milt Grumman."

"Milt Grumman?"

"That U.S. deputy marshal in the wagon, the cowpoke with the broken leg."

"It was Tate Rawson killed him."

"You saw the killing?"

"I watched. Tate pressed his gun against the side of the man's head and pulled the trigger. I saw it all."

"And then it was you who tried to kill me."

"No. I tried to miss you. I just wanted you to get hurt bad enough to put Tate off."

"You mean you aimed to miss?"

"Yes."

"You ain't that good a shot."

"Yes, he is, Mr. Long," Melissa said softly. "He's won marksmanship prizes."

Longarm looked down in some surprise at the dying man. If what he had just told Longarm was the truth, Longarm owed him—owed him a lot.

"What about J. T. Roebuck? How did he figure in the murder of the U.S. deputy?"

"When Prewitt sent a rider into town to tell him

you were out there to see Milt Grumman, he sent us after you both."

Longarm turned to Melissa. "You heard that?"

"Yes," she said. "I heard."

Clint reached up and grabbed Longarm by the arm, his fingers digging into it like talons. "Take care of Melissa. None of this was her idea. Roebuck was behind it all."

"The stolen Mormon chronicles, too?"

"Yes."

"All right. I'll do what I can to help her."

"Promise me, deputy."

"I promise."

All fight left Bolen then. He let go Longarm's arm and leaned back, his mouth sagging open loosely. Melissa let out a tiny gasp and bent to his face, smothering it with kisses—as if love could revive the dead.

But Clint Bolen was gone, his last thoughts of Melissa's welfare.

Not until the next morning did Longarm judge Melissa to be in any condition to start back with him. His hope was to overtake Rawson and his newfound ally, but he would have to be careful not to endanger Melissa. With her as a witness, there was now a damn good chance he could put both Roebuck and Tate Rawson away for a long time.

But he would have to catch them first.

And Tate was the one who would prove the most dangerous to corner. Completely recovered from his injuries, it now appeared, he would be as dangerous as a cornered wolverine. And from the look of things, Henry Polk would be no patsy, either.

Riding back through the cleft in the rock, Longarm had no difficulty cutting both men's sign. Even so, his progress was slow. Melissa was a good enough rider, but no match for Longarm. He was continually having to rein in his dun so as not to overtax her. Roebuck and his companion were heading directly back to Pine Ridge, almost in a straight line. Noting this, a warning stirred deep within Longarm, and he found himself thinking of Patricia Fields and her gold mine.

By the second day he had difficulty keeping his horse below a lope. At first the tracks of the two riders had been sharp and clear on the ground ahead of them. But the higher they got and the rockier the ground became, the more difficulty he had following their sign. On the hard, unyielding ground the hoofprints disappeared for long stretches. Longarm pressed on nevertheless—doing his best to ignore a growing, unsettling premonition of what he might expect if he did not overtake the two men soon.

It was dusk on the third day when he heard the faint rattle of gunfire ahead of him. He held up. The distant popping came again. Then it faded and was gone, its echo dying slowly. A stillness, uncanny in its completeness, fell over the mountainside.

He glanced at Melissa. "Wait for me here."

Lifting his horse to a gallop despite the treacherous terrain, Longarm soon neared a bluff overlooking Patricia Fields' mine. Dismounting, he snaked his Winchester out of its scabbard and crept to the bluff's crest and peered over. At first he saw nothing. Then he caught sight of a man on the far slope, crouching in the rocks high above the mine entrance. The distance was too great for Longarm to tell which one of the two men he was following it was.

Then he caught sight of another man in the rocks directly below him on this side of the canyon. It was Polk, the leader of the gang Longarm had wiped out. From the position of the two men, it was obvious that Pat had been chased into the mine. The gunfire he had heard earlier meant she was putting up a battle. So far she had been successful in holding off the two men.

Abruptly, Pat poked her head out of the mineshaft. Lifting her rifle, she fired across the canyon at Polk. As her rounds sang off the rocks around him, Polk returned her fire. At the same time Tate Rawson opened up on her from the rocks above the mineshaft. Pulling herself back quickly into the mine entrance, Pat disappeared from sight.

Pat was alive. That much was certain. But she could have been wounded on that last exchange—and she was trapped.

The light was fading fast. Longarm inched off the crest, ran to his horse and rode back to make sure Melissa stayed put. He found her precisely where he had left her. She had heard the sudden fusillade and was frightened. He impressed on her how important it was that she stay back and out of sight. She agreed readily.

He left her then and regained the ridge above the mine entrance. Darkness was falling rapidly. Slowly, carefully, he picked his way down the steep slope to the rocks behind which he had seen Polk crouching.

When he reached them, he found Polk gone. Glancing farther down the slope, he saw Polk on the other side of a steep wash, crouched behind its steep bank less than a hundred yards from the mine. Longarm's glance searched the slope above the mine entrance, looking for some sign of Tate Rawson. But in the darkness, he caught no indication of Tate Rawson's presence.

Longarm kept going on down the slope and dropped lightly into the wash. But as he gained its far side and approached Polk from behind, he made too much noise. Polk heard him. Alarmed, he flung himself around.

"That you, Tate?"

Longarm swung his riflestock, aiming for the man's chin. It missed by a whisker. Polk's sixgun thundered. Longarm felt the hot lead sear past his cheek. He ducked back, his feet catching on a boulder, and went crashing to the ground. Polk fired again, wildly.

"Tate!" Polk cried in a panic. "It's the deputy! He's down here!"

Longarm pushed himself upright. Polk was already scrambling for cover. An instant later he had vanished into the night. From high above a curse floated down. The sound of a horse galloping away ahead of Longarm was followed by the sound of another set of pounding hooves on the ridge far above the mine. Both sounds faded rapidly into the night.

Longarm hauled himself out of the wash and ran toward the mine entrance. "Pat!" he called. "You all right?"

"In here, Custis!"

Longarm found Pat leaning back against an over-turned wheelbarrow, her rifle on the ground. He went down on one knee beside her. A dark, growing stain covered the front of her dress. She had been shot high in the chest on the right side. Her face was gaunt, her eyes painful slits as she peered up at him through the mine tunnel's gloom.

"It was that sonofabitch in the rocks above me," she told Longarm bitterly.

"You're losing blood."

"I know that, dammit! Are they gone?"

"I'm pretty sure they are. What the hell did they want?"

"My gold. And when I got my senses and remembered your description of that fellow you told me might be tracking you, it was too late."

"Tate Rawson."

"That's the one. An ugly sonofabitch—only one eye. You didn't tell me about that."

"I don't know about it myself."

"Well," she chuckled softly. "The bastards didn't get my gold."

"Where is it?"

"It's in here. Don't worry. I got it well hid. And don't think I'm going to tell you where."

Longarm laughed, bent and took her up in his arms. She gasped in pain as he lifted her, but made no more outcry. As he carried her from the mine, she snaked her arms around his neck and leaned her head against his chest. He kissed her lightly on the fore-head. Her arms tightened gratefully around his neck, and he realized she was going to be all right.

137

He carried her carefully out of the mine, then through the darkness to her cabin.

Late the next day, with only a few hours of daylight left, Longarm caught sight of his quarry. He was cresting a hill above a long benchland. Beyond the bench lay the last jagged ramparts of the Salmon River range. Two, maybe three miles distant, two horsemen were heading for a distant pass. Soon they would be putting the mountains behind them.

Dismounting, Longarm transferred his saddle to the big chestnut he had been leading. It was the one Melissa had ridden as far at Pat's cabin. After removing the bullet from Pat's wound, Longarm had left Melissa with the wounded woman. Mounting the chestnut, he affectionately patted the dun he was leaving behind, then spurred the chestnut into the timber above the benchland, driving the horse to its limit until he had overtaken, then passed beyond, the two riders.

Cutting down through the pine-covered slope, he hauled back on the reins just before he broke from the timber and peered out. Between the approaching riders and the pass Longarm caught sight of a dry river course, the cottonwood bordering it thick with midsummer foliage. Keeping to the timber, Longarm cut behind a hillock and entered the cottonwood screening the riverbed.

He had given this matter much thought. He could not besiege the two gunmen. One would always be able to work his way around behind Longarm. And bushwhacking them both would be out of the question, since he might well get one of them, or worse, succeed only in warning them of his presence. He had settled on the one alternative he had—a sudden, frontal attack. This would take one of them out of the action immediately, the other soon after, with no chance for them to gang up on him.

With the sun a bloodshot eye resting on the horizon, Longarm sat his trembling, lathered mount and waited for Rawson and Polk to get closer. They were above him on the benchland, riding almost directly toward him. They could not see him below them in the cottonwood, but he could hear the steady drumbeat of their hooves and, as they got closer, the occasional sharp bark of their laughter.

It was a particularly loud explosion of mirth that ignited Longarm. Raking the chestnut with his spurs, he sent the big mount charging from the cottonwoods and swept up the slope on a dead run. Cresting the benchland, Longarm burst into view less than fifty yards in front of the two riders. Before the chestnut's hind hooves came down on the benchland, Longarm fired his .44 at the nearest rider, Henry Polk. He missed. Still racing toward the two riders, Longarm fired a second time. His horse shied violently away from the Colt's detonation and almost went down. Polk's own horse reared, its head catching Longarm's second slug in the jaw. The horse kept going over backward, falling onto its rider. Longarm swept past Polk and his downed, thrashing horse to follow after Tate Rawson, who had hauled his mount around the moment Longarm broke into view.

But that charge up the slope had taken most of his horse's reserves. The horse stumbled drunkenly and almost went down. Longarm hauled on the reins and kept the animal on its feet, and with a fierce, loud cry, startled the chestnut into one more burst of speed. With nothing left but heart, it kept going. Longarm could hear it rasping painfully for breath, and its headlong run was getting ragged and wobbly. With his knees and the reins, Longarm lifted the horse over a gentle rise. But on the far side the horse stumbled, and this time Longarm could not drag its head up. Its front feet went out from under it, and it struck with its head out straight and crunched down jaw-first into the ground. As it flopped over on its side, Longarm was flung headlong over its neck. He rolled once, regained his feet, and darted back to the downed horse.

Snaking his rifle out of the exposed sling, he whirled and knelt on one knee, intent only on hitting Tate Rawson's horse. He tracked the fleeing rider, lifted the rifle some to allow for distance, and squeezed off a shot. It missed. He levered a fresh round into the chamber, kept himself grimly calm, and tracked the horse and rider again. Squeezing off his second shot, he jumped to his feet and watched as the horse pitched forward, catapulting Tate Rawson over its head. Scrambling to his feet, Rawson limped painfully into a patch of birch trees, lugging his rifle.

Longarm raced after him.

It was almost pitch-dark by the time he flung himself down behind the dead horse Rawson had left and began pouring a steady fire into the thin stand of birches, the fusillade of hot lead smacking into trees and shearing off branches. After a few moments, Longarm got to his feet. Levering and firing steadily, he raced the remaining distance to the birches, his rapid fire cutting a withering swath before him.

Plunging into the inky darkness of the birch stand, he heard a scream of rage as a deafening gunshot roared to his left. The round smacked into a tree just above his head. Longarm flung himself in the direction from which the shot had come. Levering a fresh round into the firing chamber, he squeezed the trigger. The hammer came down on an empty chamber. Without pause, Longarm flipped the rifle in his hand. As a second shot roared up at him from the ground, he clubbed down at the barely visible form crouched in the tangle of underbrush.

He felt the stock strike flesh and bone and heard the cry that came with it. He flung himself onto the figure below him and tried to wrest the .45 from Tate Rawson's hand. The weapon detonated. Longarm felt exploding gunpowder singe his cheek as the slug burned past. He did not let go the .45, but continued to twist it. There was another detonation.

"Oh, Jesus! I'm hit!" Rawson cried.

Longarm pulled back and saw Rawson crawling swiftly, frantically away from him into the trees. Longarm lunged after him, picked him up by the scruff of his neck and flung him to one side. Rawson rolled over once and slammed with sickening force against a tree trunk. When he shook himself groggily and tried to get up, Longarm kicked him in the ass, driving him headfirst into a tree. Gasping, Rawson fell to the ground.

Fighting for breath, his face streaked with sweat, Longarm looked down at the slowly twisting body at his feet. A black sea of exhaustion washed over him.

Every muscle in his body was made of wet cotton. There was a roaring in his ears. Collapsing to one knee, he reached a hand out to grab a tree trunk until the sound faded. Then he heard the pounding footsteps coming up behind him.

Polk was free of that thrashing horse!

Longarm turned. A gun detonated. A flash of powder lanced toward him through the darkness. The bullet struck him high on his left shoulder, spinning him around and slamming him to the ground. He heard Polk crashing through the underbrush toward him. A kick in his side flung him onto his back. He saw Polk's dim figure standing over him. Tate Rawson was on his feet now and had joined him. Even in the darkness of the trees, Longarm could see the bastard's eager grin.

Longarm lifted his .44. Polk lashed out with his foot, kicking the gun from his grasp. Moaning loudly, Longarm rolled over, palming his derringer. He kept rolling. On his back again, he saw Polk aiming his sixgun carefully down at him.

Longarm fired the derringer up at him. Shifting his aim slightly, he fired a second round, blowing off the top of Tate Rawson's head. Polk went down on one knee, his hand clutching at his gut. He was mewling in pain. Longarm pushed himself slowly to his feet and looked over at Rawson. Tate was flat on his back, his skull resting in a black puddle.

It was over—so far.

But there still remained J. T. Roebuck, the author of this grisly feast.

Chapter Nine

"What happened to you?" Pat cried, as Longarm slumped against the doorjamb, a weak smile on his face.

"I got hit."

It had taken Longarm much longer to get back to the mine than it had taken him to overtake the two men. He had managed to dig out the bullet, after which he had passed out and, during his slumber, nearly bled himself white. When he came to, he was as weak as a kitten, and it was a long time before he found the dun he had left behind when he changed over to the chestnut.

"Here," Melissa cried, jumping up from the table and hurrying to his side, "let me help you!"

Longarm let her lead him to the cot. Fully dressed, but with a blanket on her lap and a fresh cup of coffee in her hand, Patricia was sitting up in a chair at the table. As Melissa eased him down onto the cot, he glanced over at Pat and noticed how much better she looked. And Melissa, too. Her puffed lips were back to normal, and the bruises on her face and neck were nearly gone. Pat got up from her chair to join Melissa at Longarm's side.

"I already took the bullet out," Longarm told Pat. "I just need to rest up some."

"Them two animals," Pat said. "Did you get them?"

Longarm nodded.

"Both?" Melissa asked, her eyes wide.

"Yes."

Pat leaned forward impulsively and planted a kiss on his forehead. "That's a good boy," she said. "You deserve a reward."

"I deserve a rest first."

"Yes. Then a reward."

It came in less than two weeks, on a hot, sultry night when Longarm awakened to the rustling of his bed-sheets as Pat slipped in beside him. The cabin was too crowded for two healthy women and a man, so Longarm had been sleeping on a straw mattress in the small horse-barn. The bright moonlight streaming in through the single window over his mattress gave him enough light to see her clearly.

"You sure you're up to this?" Longarm asked her.

Pat reached down and felt his growing member. "Just so long as you are, Custis."

Leaning over him, she caressed his face gently as he took in the wonder of her long, dark hair cascading down past her shoulders and coiling about her firm, upthrust breasts. At moments such as this, she was not an old woman. The puckered scar where he had probed for the bullet Tate had sent into her was still visible; but it was healing so well he barely noticed it.

Murmuring happily, Pat took his face in her hands, leaned closer, and kissed him on the mouth. Her lips opened and, as her tongue found his, she flung her arms around his neck and ground her naked body hard against him.

Longarm brought his hand up to cup her warm breast. His rough fingertips caressed the nipple. He heard her groan, her arms still about his neck, her tongue still probing deliciously. His head began to spin with his need for her. He could smell her. It was the aroma of a woman fully aroused, and was a thousand times more exciting than any perfume.

He broke the kiss and took one of her nipples in his mouth. It swelled and became as hard as a bullet. His tongue flicked it expertly. Pat leaned back, moaning softly, then reached down hungrily for his crotch and grabbed him, pulling his engorged penis toward her. Opening her legs she strained toward him. Longarm's probing hand found her pubic patch, then her moist, pliant lips. Groaning in anticipation, she thrust herself under him and spread her legs wider. With his big hand he held her buttocks up as he leaned heavily and entered, plowing deep.

"Ah!" she cried softly, and flung her head back, bringing up her legs and locking her ankles around the back of his neck.

"Deeper, Custis!" she commanded huskily.

It was a familiar cry, and Longarm did his best to comply. He pulled out of her, leaving just the tip of his erection within her outer lips, then plunged back into her powerfully, sounding deep, impaling her on the mattress. She uttered a sharp, guttural cry that seemed to be wrung from the deepest part of her. Her ankles tightened convulsively around his neck. Again and again, he drove into her, going deeper, it seemed, with each incredible thrust.

"Yes! Yes!" she cried, flinging her head back and forth wildly. "Yes, yes. Oh, that's it! Don't stop now!"

Longarm smiled grimly. He had no intention of stopping now. He increased his pace and the depth of his thrusts until she shuddered and began hammering him furiously on the shoulders. Crying out intensely, she climaxed, erupting wildly under him. She was like a human earthquake opening up beneath him and pulling him into her. As her cry became a wail, he felt himself losing control as well. He could hold back no longer and was suddenly over the edge, hammering down upon her, then exploding titanically inside her—again and again and again.

Dazedly, he lifted off her at last and gazed fondly down at her face, shiny now with perspiration.

"How was that?"

"Mmmm," she said.

He relaxed forward onto her glistening body, aware that he was still large within her. Still panting softly, she straightened her legs and hugged him tightly to keep him inside her; then, to his astonishment, she mounted him smoothly from the top, thrusting backward onto him, gasping with pleasure as she felt his shaft plunging deep within her. Squeezing delightedly with the muscles in her vagina, she began to rotate her hips slowly, maddeningly.

Longarm lay back and let her have her way with him. She knew precisely what she was doing and what it took to set her off. Prolonging the pleasure of it as much as was humanly possible, she paused in her rotating movements for shorter and shorter periods until at last she succumbed to her own mounting pleasure. While her long hair streamed down over Longarm's face and shoulders, she began rocking wildly back and forth until once more—with deep, guttural groans of pleasure—she climaxed, pouring her juices down over him in a hot, delicious explosion.

Limp, gasping, she fell forward upon his chest and lay there, trembling. Longarm, meanwhile, had held himself back, intent only on seeing to it that he remained large enough for her to pleasure herself on top of him. Now he pulled her over and rolled on top of her, as hot now as a five-dollar pistol.

"Again?" she cried. "So soon? Do you think you can manage it, Custis?"

"Don't you worry about me none," he told her eagerly. "Just lay back and let it happen."

She allowed herself a deep, warm chuckle. "Just as you say, Custis."

He was already thrusting with full, slow, even strokes, determined not to hurry. He was, after all, convalescing from a bullet wound. He had told her to lie back and relax, and that is just what she did for the first few minutes. She was still short of breath from her own wild ride of a moment before, but gradually she came to life under him—as he knew she would.

Longarm felt her inner muscles responding to his measured, metronomic thrusts. She began to meet his downward thrusts with upward thrusts of her own—and then to respond faster, and drive up at him still harder. Tiny cries of delight escaped her. She kept her eyes shut tightly and her head began to snap back and forth.

Longarm was on his own now, building to the final moment. It had been a long time coming for both of them, but by this time their bodies had taken over, and with a mounting fierceness, they slammed at each other relentlessly, giving no quarter and asking none. He pounded on with fast, repeated, driving thrusts until he could hear Pat's short, startled grunts. Her body pulsed with his as she drew him deeper and deeper into her. Then she arched her back, crying out in a wild sob. Longarm felt himself pulsing out of control as well, emptying, throbbing—until he was drained completely.

He dropped upon her, gasping, his face resting on the hot, sweaty warmth of her breasts, spent utterly. When their breathing had quieted at last, Pat ran her fingers through his damp hair.

"That was lovely, Custis," she murmured happily. "But I couldn't just lie still and let it happen."

He grinned. "I didn't think you would be able to do that, either. I just wanted you to relax."

"You know much about women, Custis."

"Maybe so."

"And I know much about men. We make a good team."

"We both sure know how to get ourselves shot up."

"But you're all mended now, Custis."

"And so are you."

"Will you be going back soon?"

"Yes."

"How soon?"

"Tomorrow, I guess."

"I will miss you."

"With all that gold, you should take a trip."

"Where do you suggest, Custis?"

"Paris."

"Why Paris?"

"I understand the Parisians appreciate older, experienced women."

"Is that what I am?"

"Yes."

"And do you appreciate me?"

"What do you think?"

She pondered a while, her hand still stroking his hair. "Maybe I'll do that," she said, musingly. "Go to Paris, I mean. I've got enough. More than enough, if it comes to that."

He kissed her on the lips. She kissed him back eagerly, then pushed herself erect. She had hung her nightgown on a nail. Taking it down, she let it fall over her like a shimmering white cloud. Then, with a quick wave, she vanished out the door.

Her light, running footsteps faded. He sighed contentedly and rolled over, a blessed, empty fatigue settling over him like a benediction. He was asleep almost at once and would have slept until late that next morning if someone had not pulled him from his sleep. It was like he was under water and was being dragged back to the surface.

When his eyes opened, he saw Melissa bent over him, her naked breasts inches from his face.

"I came to you," she whispered. "I wanted to thank you."

"Thank me?"

"Yes."

"For what?"

"You'll clear my name for me, won't you?"

"That was my intention—for cooperating."

"Oh, I'll cooperate, Custis. I told you I would."

"You don't need to thank me, Melissa."

"But . . . I want to."

He couldn't believe it. Glancing past her out through the window, he saw that it was close to dawn. But his limbs were like lead and that which hung between his legs had no more substance than a piece of wet macaroni.

"Please, Melissa. My wound . . . it still bothers me. Whenever I turn or lift anything. I'm sorry. Perhaps later, when I'm better . . . after we reach Pine Ridge."

"Pine Ridge?"

"Yes. We'll be leaving tomorrow."

"You mean you want to wait that long?"

"If I have to, Melissa."

She leaned still closer, her incandescent breasts almost smothering him, then took his lips with hers. At that moment, he wondered if she could really have been entirely innocent in all that business with her late husband and the Mormon chronicles. Certainly her period of mourning should have been a mite longer.

In mourning or not, for what seemed like a delicious eternity, her lips held his. Incredibly, he felt himself stirring to life. Then, releasing his lips, Melissa turned and vanished out the door. Watching her leave, he realized she had come all the way from the cabin without a stitch of clothing on.

Wearily, he pulled the blanket over his shoulders and closed his eyes. As he plunged into sleep, his last thought was pure astonishment that for the first time he could remember he had turned down a beautiful, naked woman. He comforted himself with the knowledge that he would have a chance to make amends for that failing when he and Melissa reached Pine Ridge—if not sooner.

Four days later, Longarm and Melissa checked into the Cosmopolitan Hotel in Pine Ridge. They got in around noon. After eating their lunch in the hotel dining room, Longarm checked Melissa into a room of her own, after which he left the hotel to visit Sheriff Bond.

He found Bond sitting out on the small porch in front of his office, his wooden chair leaning back against the wall, his long legs crossed as they rested on the railing. He had a lit cheroot in his mouth. He offered one to Longarm as Longarm pulled a chair over and sat down beside him.

Longarm thanked him, bit off the cheroot's end, and lit up. The traffic in the street was heavy, the clop of hoofs and the rattle of wagons filling the late afternoon. They watched it for a while in silence.

"See you brought back the redhead," Bond said finally.

"Yep."

"What about Clint?"

"He's back where I found him. Ever hear of the Polk gang?"

"The Polk gang? You mean Henry Polk?"

"That's the one."

"Hell, yes. I got some dodgers in there on them. California bunch, ain't they?"

"Was."

Bond turned his head to look at Longarm, then took the cheroot out of his mouth. "What happened?"

Longarm told him.

When he had finished, Bond looked back at the street, lit his cheroot up again and shook his head slowly. "Roebuck's up here."

Longarm felt himself quicken.

"He's out at his ranch, the Circle R. He rode in yesterday with his foreman."

"Prewitt?"

"That's right."

"Well now, that's going to save me a trip."

"Figured you'd be pleased."

"Maybe you and me could take a ride out this afternoon. Give Roebuck the good news."

"What good news?"

"That Melissa has sworn to tell all she knows in a court of law—that if Roebuck doesn't come in quietly, I'm going to swear out a warrant for his arrest."

"Arrest? What for?"

"For the theft of those Mormon documents and complicity in the murder of a U.S. deputy and the attempted murder of another."

"Who's another?"

"Me."

"I don't know what jurisdiction I got for all that, Long. Besides, if he wants to, Roebuck has enough money to buy every lawyer and judge in this territory."

"He already has, Bond. He'll have little to worry about if he just stays put."

Bond nodded. Longarm could see he understood. Longarm was about to beat the bushes, do his best to unsettle his quarry. No one looked more guilty than a man in flight from the law. If Longarm could flush Roebuck, a lot of confusion over jurisdiction would vanish. A federal warrant could be issued, one good in every state and territory.

"Meet me back here in half an hour," Bond said, getting to his feet. Longarm nodded and left the porch.

"You're going out to see Mr. Roebuck? Now?"

"Yes, Melissa."

"I'm frightened."

"Don't be. He doesn't know I'm back yet—and he knows nothing of what happened."

"He's a terrible man, Custis."

"And powerful. I know all that. But once I get him on the run, he'll be just another criminal."

"I'm still afraid."

"Don't be. Now, what can you tell me about this

153

Prewitt, his foreman? I met him once before, but I don't know much about him."

"He takes orders, like anyone else—according to what Clint told me. I met him when Clint bought the cattle in Kansas."

"He knows you?"

"Well enough to know me on sight."

"Stay downstairs in the lobby or out on the hotel porch, in plain sight, until I get back," Longarm told her.

"Why?"

"Just do it."

"You think he'll come after me."

"I didn't say that."

"You didn't have to say it. I know the man—and how he thinks."

"If you stay in sight, you'll be perfectly safe."

"Until you get back, you mean."

"I'm sorry, Melissa. There's no other way. Don't forget it was he who sent Tate Rawson after you and Clint."

"I am not forgetting that, Custis."

Longarm took his hat up from the bed and clapped it on. "I'll escort you downstairs."

"There's no need for that."

"As you wish."

As Longarm opened the door, she called his name. He turned and looked back at her.

"Be careful. Roebuck's a snake."

Longarm nodded and pulled the door shut behind him and headed down the stairs.

* * *

Tim Prewitt's blocky figure burst through the doorway. Irritated, Roebuck glanced up from his desk. "Dammit! I got work to do, Prewitt. What do you want?"

"You got visitors, J. T."

"Visitors? Speak plain, man! Who?"

"That deputy U.S. marshal and Sheriff Bond."

"The hell you say!"

"Come and see for yourself."

"Get the boys!"

As Prewitt left Roebuck's office, Roebuck reached for the bottle of laudanum he now kept by him at all times. He used his left hand, since his right wrist, though no longer in a cast, was not yet strong. He took a healthy belt of the laudanum, felt much better instantly, and hurried from the office.

Standing beside Prewitt on the porch a moment later, Roebuck watched as Sheriff Bond rode in beside the deputy U.S. marshal. Where the hell was Tate Rawson? he asked himself. This tall drink of water should be a dead man. Tate was one rattlesnake of a human being, as deadly and tenacious as a chest cold in the winter. The thought that this deputy marshal might have somehow bested Tate Rawson caused a sinking feeling in the pit of Roebuck's stomach. Nor was Sheriff Bond any to his liking, either. Bond had boasted he couldn't be bought—and so far Roebuck had been unable to do so.

So now Roebuck was facing two honest men in the same afternoon.

It was an unsettling prospect, and Roebuck was

pleased at the sight of his men heading toward the big house from all directions. But what the hell was the matter with him? What did he have to worry about? He still had all the cards, didn't he? No one could touch him—not in this territory or anyplace else.

The two lawmen halted their mounts a few yards back of the hitchrail. It was Bond who spoke.

"Howdy, Mr. Roebuck."

"What brings you out here, Bond?"

Roebuck had decided to ignore the sonofabitch sitting in his saddle beside him.

"This here gent beside me is U.S. Deputy Marshal Custis Long," Bond told Roebuck. "He'd like to have a word with you, if you don't mind."

"I mind plenty. I already know the sonofabitch."

"Well, then, I'll let him say his piece."

By this time Roebuck's men were standing in a semicircle around the two riders. There were so many they were almost two deep, and every man jack of them hand-picked riders who were used to following orders, no matter what those orders were as long as the one who issued them paid well and on time. Roebuck did both.

"I'm listening," Roebuck snapped.

"Unless you come with me quietly, Roebuck," the deputy U.S. Marshal said, "I'll have Bond here swear out a warrant for your arrest."

"A warrant?"

"For the murder of Milt Grumman."

"You must be joking! What proof you got that I had anything to do with that?"

"Clint Bolen's wife will testify to her husband's

confession before he died. He was with Tate Rawson, your hireling, when Tate killed Grumman."

"Tate?"

"That's right."

"Where is Tate? He's the one you want, not me."

"Tate was killed resisting arrest."

Roebuck felt a funny taste in his mouth—like rust. Or was it the taste of death? Fear swept over him. Worse, a nameless dread. Oh, God, if only he could get himself another swig of that laudanum now!

"Well, then," he heard himself say to the U.S. marshal, surprised at the raw arrogance in his voice, "if Tate Rawson's dead, then that ends it."

"Not if you were the one behind Milt Grumman's death," the marshal told him coldly.

"How you going to prove that, lawman?"

"I told you. Bolen's widow."

"You think a jury will believe her?"

"Why shouldn't they?"

"She'd only be lying to clear her husband."

"Then why don't we let a jury decide that, Roebuck? You may be right. You may walk away from this, cleared of all involvement in Milt Grumman's murder. Come with me now and your cooperation will go a long ways to clearing your name."

"Go with you?"

"Sure. We promise that no harm will come to you. You'll be free on bond in a matter of days."

"You must be out of your head! I'm not comin' with you!"

"Is that your last word on it?"

"You're goddamn right it is! Get off this ranch! Both of you!"

"You refuse to come with me."

"If you and Bond don't pull out now, I'll have you both blasted from your saddles."

As he spoke, several of his men drew their six-guns, while others raised their rifles. They were waiting for Roebuck's orders—and were perfectly willing to carry them out.

"You threatening the law, Roebuck?" Sheriff Bond asked, his voice hard, his eyes fixing Roebuck's like two gunbarrels.

Roebuck knew he was not thinking clearly. He knew it, but there was nothing he could do to prevent it. All he wanted was for these two men to get off his land. And if not that, he wanted them dead. He would not go to any prison cell, no matter for how long. Not for one instant.

"You heard me, Sheriff," Roebuck said, his mouth dry, his voice shaking. "I won't bother to repeat it. Both of you ride out of here. Now."

With a quick, curt nod, Bond wheeled his horse, the U.S. marshal following his example. As the two men's horses cut through the ranks of grim Circle R men, Roebuck had a momentary urge to scream at his men to cut down these two damn fools.

He did not do it only because he knew his men would do just what he said. And then he would be responsible. Just as he was responsible for the death of that deputy! Groaning inwardly, Roebuck turned and fled back into the house, anxious to reach his office—and that waiting bottle of laudanum.

"Prewitt!" he bleated. "Get in here!"

Snatching up the laudanum, he gulped its contents down and flung the empty bottle into his wastebasket. There was, he knew, another bottle waiting for him in his desk drawer.

As Prewitt came to a halt in front of his desk, Roebuck looked bleakly up at him.

"You heard the sonofabitch. Melissa's alive. And she's willing to spill her guts to the law. I want her taken care of."

"Taken care of?"

"Dammit! You know what I want."

"You want her killed."

"I'll put you in charge of it. Get this done for me, Prewitt, and you'll never want for another thing as long as you live."

"What'll you give me, Mr. Roebuck?"

"That spread I signed over to Bolen."

"Them Watts brothers own it now, Mr. Roebuck —and an army trained in hell couldn't wedge them off it. No, sir. That won't be much of a reward for killing Melissa."

"What's your price, dammit?"

"This spread here. The Circle R. I've worked it for six years now. I know it like the palm of my hand. You only show up here once in a while. You got railroads to run—and if I know you, you'll be in Washington one of these days. Let me have this spread."

"Done! You just take care of Melissa. Do you know any men you can trust with this?"

"Three, besides myself."

"Then do it, Prewitt. Do it before another day

passes. I want that girl out of my hair. Without her as a witness, there's nothing can tie me to any killin'."

Prewitt smiled coldly. "I'll get my horse saddled and speak to the men I got in mind. Then I'll stop by here and pick up a bill of sale for this ranch. You can say I paid five thousand for it. That's a good price."

"Get your men and get back here. I'll have the bill of sale ready. Now move!"

As Prewitt left the room, Roebuck dove into his drawer and, with shaking hands, pulled out the unopened bottle of laudanum. He almost cried when he spilled a few drops after unscrewing the cap.

Chapter Ten

When Longarm and Bond rode into Pine Ridge, Bond stopped at his office while Longarm kept on to the hotel. Dismounting in front of it, he caught sight of Melissa sitting on a wicker chair on the hotel porch. She seemed relieved to see him and got immediately to her feet. Longarm dropped his reins over the hitchrail and mounted the porch steps. She greeted him eagerly and they went inside. Longarm picked up the key to his room, then went back to her.

"I think you'd better get the key to your room, too," he told her.

"Of course, Custis."

As soon as she got it from the desk clerk, they ascended the stairs to the second floor, where he took her key and gave her his own key in exchange.

"I want you to stay in my room tonight," he ex-

161

plained. "Transfer what you'll need from your room to mine; then we'll go down for supper."

"Your room? I don't understand."

"You'll be safer there, and I'll see if I can get some sleep in yours."

"You expect someone to come for me. And you'll be waiting in my place when they do."

"Melissa, do what I said. Get your things. Quickly now."

He walked down the hall to her room and opened it, then waited while she picked up her small carpetbag, gathered up the few personal items she had left out on the top of the dresser, then moved back out of the room. He closed the door behind her and followed her up the stairs to the third floor and opened the door to his room for her.

Inside, she put her things down, then spun about and sat down on the bed to face him. Her face was pale, drawn. "I'm scared."

"No need to be."

"Suppose Roebuck comes after you—not me?"

"I thought of that. Sheriff Bond will be in here—just in case."

"And you'll be downstairs in my room, alone?"

"Yes."

"This is crazy."

"I got Roebuck very frightened and very desperate, Melissa. He doesn't want to go to jail—not even for a short stay. So right now, he's not thinking very clearly."

She shuddered. "Let's eat, then."

He smiled, considering that request a healthy reaction.

The three gunslicks Prewitt had chosen were recent additions to the Circle R crew. Prewitt had hired each one.

Jed Degnan was a small, bluff fellow with a cheery, raw face, bad teeth, and a love of Irish whiskey—morning, noon, and night. As far as Prewitt could determine, however, it had no effect on his ability to function. His well-oiled Remington sidearm was always in top condition, and he could hit a fly on a fencepost at fifty paces. At the moment, riding beside Prewitt, Degnan was taking small, medicinal sips from a silver flask he had taken from one of his saddle bags.

Tom Willow was Prewitt's second choice, a narrow-jawed fox of a man with light, hazel eyes that burned with a peculiar intensity. Slim, tall, without an ounce of extra tallow on his frame, he ate like a bird—that is, all the time.

Riding alongside him at the moment was Bigger Rust. As his name implied, Bigger was an oversized hulk of a man with more muscle than brain. He took orders without question, and did not have enough sense, it seemed, to know fear. He was good enough with a gun, but better with his hands. Close in, Prewitt would rather tackle a grizzly than this man. Bearded, with small, black eyes and dark brows, he looked as dangerous as he was.

Tom Willow was more than Bigger's friend; he was Bigger's keeper. Bigger kept close to Willow because he knew the smaller man had the judgment he lacked, and Willow obviously depended on the muscle Bigger supplied.

These three men Prewitt was counting on to finish off not only Melissa but that fool of a U.S. marshal as well. This might not have been Roebuck's intent, but Prewitt knew what he was doing. He had no intention of taking part in any gunplay, and when the fireworks began he would be back at the Circle R.

The way Prewitt figured it Roebuck, not Prewitt, would be the one who had to take the heat. Though Roebuck had more than enough pull to keep himself out of jail, he was now a fullblown opium addict. In his present condition he would be unable to stand up to any scrutiny, and the resulting notoriety would be enough to send him packing from this territory.

And that would leave Prewitt with the ranch he had always coveted.

It was a little past sundown when the four men rode into Pine Ridge. Dismounting in front of the town's biggest saloon, they entered and found a table at the rear. They ordered a round, and, after clearing some of the dust from his tonsils, Prewitt left the others and crossed the street to the hotel.

Spinning a gold piece on the front desk's blotter, he smiled amiably at the desk clerk. "You got a fellow registered here name of Custis Long?"

"We do."

"And his girlfriend, Melissa?"

"I was not aware they were anything more than acquaintances."

"Are they here?"

The desk clerk hesitated. Prewitt slapped a second gold piece down onto the blotter. The clerk took it and cleared his throat. "Yes, they are registered."

"I'd like their room numbers."

The clerk looked around nervously, reluctant to respond to this kind of grilling on the hotel's guests. It just wasn't done.

"Mr. Roebuck's coming to visit them later this evening," Prewitt explained with a wink, leaning forward confidentially. "To visit the girl, anyway. He might stop in later to see his old friend, Mr. Long."

"I see." The clerk picked up the second coin. "The girl's in room two-ten and Mr. Long is in room three-twenty."

"Much obliged."

Prewitt dropped a third coin onto the desk and left the lobby, satisfied that he had said and done enough to implicate Roebuck.

Returning to the saloon, he rejoined the three men and ordered another round. Then he explained precisely what he had in mind for them. When he had finished, there was a nervous silence. For an awkward moment, Prewitt wondered if he might not have misjudged these three men. Perhaps they were not of a caliber capable of carrying out such a bold—if bloodthirsty—stroke.

"Sounds good to me," said Jed Degnan, leaning back suddenly, a cold smile on his face. He cocked his head at Prewitt. "You say you'll give each of us a couple of hundred?"

"That's what I said."

"And all we have to do is finish off the U.S. marshal and the red-headed dame?"

Prewitt nodded.

"Make it five hundred for me. What these other two get is up to them."

"We'll take five hundred each, too," said Tom Willow. "We don't go around killin' people for nothing." He turned to Bigger. "Ain't that right, Bigger?"

"Sure is, Tom."

"You heard 'em, Prewitt," Degnan said, grinning. "That's five hundred for each of us—or no deal."

Prewitt shrugged and quickly nodded his agreement. He had been willing to go as high as a thousand apiece.

"Now here's how it should go," he told them quietly. "I already told you their room numbers. Wait until after midnight, visit their rooms and let them have it. Use knives. They're quieter. But blast them if you have to. I figure it would be smart to split up your targets. Jed, you could take Melissa. Tom and Bigger should be enough to handle the deputy. Leave your horses down in the alley back of the hotel. When you finish, go down the back stairs and ride out of town."

"And when we do, it looks like we won't be lookin' back," Degnan said. "So I guess maybe you'll be paying us before we perform this little chore. Ain't that right, Prewitt?"

"Fair enough. The money's in my saddlebags. I'll bring it right in."

"Not here," said Tom Willow, his eyes narrow. "Outside."

"Suits me."

The four men got up from the table and went outside to their horses. Unlacing his saddlebag, Prewitt carried it into the shadows of a nearby alley and distributed the banknotes Roebuck had given him when he handed over the phony bill of sale for the Circle

R. Jed and Tom Willow counted the money carefully. Tom Willow, as Prewitt had expected, took Bigger's share for safekeeping.

Prewitt returned to his horse then, mounted up, and rode out of town, heading back to the Circle R.

Longarm had watched in some surprise when Prewitt left town earlier. He had not seen him enter Pine Ridge, and was surprised to see the man riding out. But that didn't mean anything, Longarm realized. Prewitt could ride back in later that night and make his move. That Roebuck would make a move against Melissa seemed inescapable. The man had no choice. Prewitt—or Roebuck himself—would return when everyone was asleep. Sometime after midnight, Longarm had reckoned.

Now it was close to midnight. Slumped back against the wall in a corner facing the bed, Longarm peered intently at the cunningly contrived dummy he had fashioned in the bed. He had even gone to the extreme of purchasing a wig of red hair, and spilling the fake tresses over the coverlet. It was strange, but even though Longarm knew it was a fake, at times he fancied he could see the gentle rise and fall of the dummy's breast as it slept.

It would do the trick, all right.

Midnight came and went. The traffic in the street below quieted. At last only a single horse could be heard clopping off down the street, heading out of town.

For a long while Longarm waited. A girl's laugh came from a floor below. Somewhere in the hotel a door slammed. Then silence, complete and utter, fell over the hotel. Longarm was about to stand up and go to the window when he heard a board creak outside the door. He froze. The soft clash of a skeleton key in the door's lock caused him to draw his .44. The door opened a crack and a man slipped into the room.

Longarm could smell the whiskey on the man from where he sat, but the fellow was not the slightest bit unsteady as he approached the bed. In his left hand he held a long Remington revolver, in his right a knife—a bowie judging from the heft of its blade. Good idea—a knife to keep things quiet, a gun if anything went awry.

Longarm watched the assassin move to the side of the bed and then, in one terrible, downward stroke, plunge the knife into the dummy. Longarm stood up.

"Hold it right there, mister!" he commanded.

The man whirled and flung up his revolver. Longarm fired. The would-be assasin appeared to hang suspended for a moment. Longarm saw his revolver swing up. He fired a second time. The man's head snapped back, his body following it. He thumped heavily to the floor.

Longarm sprinted over to the man and looked down at him. He had never seen him before. Prewitt was keeping his hands clean, and had hired someone to do Roebuck's dirty work for him. Aware that the gunfire would draw a crowd of guests, he hurried from the room to assure Melissa and Bond that they could relax now. Running lightly down the hallway, he turned up the stairs. He was on the third floor landing when he heard a scream from inside his room followed by two muffled explosions.

Two men charged from his room, the one in front followed closely by an astonishing bear of a man. At the sight of Longarm, both men flung up their revolvers and fired. Longarm dove to the floor as the slugs slammed into the plaster behind him. The two men raced down the hallway, heading for the rear stairs. Longarm fired carefully at the big one and caught him in the back. He went down, giving Longarm a clear shot at the smaller one. His last bullet caught this one before he could make the rear stairs. He stumbled, then sprawled face down on the floor.

Longarm got back up and raced into his room. On the floor behind the bed he found Melissa, naked as a plucked chicken, a knife protruding from her right breast. Bond, just as naked, was on the floor beside the bed, two bullets in his back. One had apparently severed his spine.

Longarm rolled him over as gently as possible. Bond's eyes flickered open.

"What the hell happened?" Longarm asked.

Bond frowned, then grinned ironically. "We . . . Melissa and I . . . were hard at it, Long. Maybe . . . too hard."

Bond's eyes closed then, the ironic grin becoming a hard, fatal grimace. Longarm swore bitterly, unable to believe the extent of his miscalculation. He heard a growing murmur in the doorway and the sound of boots thumping up the stairs. Glancing over, he saw a growing crowd jamming the room's open doorway.

Through the crowd pushed Bond's deputy, his gun out. A look of pure shock appeared on his face when he caught sight of the sheriff's still body sprawled on the floor. Bond had stationed him in the lobby as a backup. It hadn't done much good.

Pushing himself past the deputy, Longarm hurried down the hallway to the big man he had caught from behind. Barely conscious, the killer was lying face down. Longarm's slug had hit him high on the shoulder, burying itself in his muscle. It was not in the least fatal.

Longarm turned the man over and bent over his bearded face. "Who put you up to this?" he demanded.

The big man's arm swung up, caught Longarm on the side of the head and slammed him back against the wall. Dazed, Longarm tried to shake off the effects of the blow. When he did, he caught sight of the man vanishing down the back stairs. Jumping over the other one lying in a pool of his own blood, Longarm plunged after him down the stairs. The killer broke out into the alley ahead of him. Longarm heard the sharp, sudden pound of hoofs as the man galloped off. Longarm pushed through the door into the alley and for a long, weary moment stood in the alley listening to the fading hoofbeats.

Then he reentered the hotel. He didn't really need that killer's testimony as to who was behind this. He already knew that only too well. Roebuck and his foreman, Tim Prewitt.

And it was time now to bring them in.

Chapter Eleven

Prewitt looked down at the wounded giant of a man sprawled on the foot of the porch steps, then turned to look at Roebuck. The owner of the Circle R was as furious as he—but unsteady, wild-eyed, close to panic.

"Damn you, Bigger," Roebuck cried. "What do you mean, you don't know?"

Bigger was close to tears. "We thought it was the deputy with the woman. But we was wrong. It was Sheriff Bond!"

"What about that U.S. deputy?" Prewitt demanded. "Did you get him?"

"No! He's the one killed Tom! He must've killed Jed, too!"

Roebuck turned to his foreman. "Goddammit,

Prewitt. Now you'll have to deal with the deputy. I don't want him comin' near me."

Prewitt nodded grimly. Though he hated to admit it, and would have done anything to prevent this showdown, Roebuck was right. It was now up to him personally to stop that U.S. marshal.

Prewitt looked back down at Bigger Rust. His back and right side was slick from the blood he had lost. That he had been able to ride this far through the night to give them as clear an account as he had was a tribute to his amazing, bull-like strength. But he appeared now to be at the end of his tether. Prewitt felt no pity at all for him, only wonder that he had lasted this long.

"Get over to the bunkhouse," he told Bigger. "See to that wound. And tell the rest of the crew to get over here. We got a visitor comin', more than likely."

Roebuck looked at Prewitt in pure dismay. "My God, Prewitt! You think he'll be comin' tonight?"

"Sure. And if he does, he'll be playing right into our hands."

"But—!"

"Don't worry, boss. He'll never get past our men."

"But we just can't shoot him!"

"You got a better idea? He just shot two of our men, didn't he? We'll only be defending ourselves. This is our ranch, don't forget. Private property. And it's dark. How would we know who was coming at us—or why?"

Roebuck's knees seemed to buckle. He nodded unhappily, the tip of his tongue moistening his dry lips. "If you say so."

"Go on inside, J.T. I'll handle this."

"Sure," Roebuck said eagerly. "You do that, Prewitt. If you need me, I'll be inside in my office. Waiting."

Prewitt watched Roebuck vanish inside, not bothering to mask the contempt he felt for the man who had once inspired such fear in all those around him. That laudanum was sure as hell powerful stuff.

He looked down at Bigger. The man had not gotten up as he had told him to. He was still sprawled face down on the steps, apparently unconscious. Moving down the steps, Prewitt shook the big man awake.

"Get off these steps," Prewitt told him. "You can't stay here."

"I . . . can't move. I'm . . . tired."

"Go on inside then. Get out of sight."

Nodding dumbly, the big man pushed himself erect and stumbled up the stairs. Prewitt watched him disappear inside, then turned and hurried across the compound toward the bunkhouse. His men were inclined to grumble, and he wasn't as sure of them as he would like to be—but he would countenance no holding back now.

The moon was a large, baleful eye hanging over Longarm's right shoulder, casting a bright sheen over the fields and sparse woodlands through which he rode. Since leaving Pine Ridge, he had kept his dun to a steady lope, and now, as he topped a rise, he saw ahead of him the Circle R buildings. The big house was a large, two-story building, fronted by a long verandah. The outbuildings included a separate

173

mess, a large bunkhouse, what looked like the dairy, and a blacksmith's shop. It was a miniature village set in a lush, grass-carpeted valley, surrounded by high, rolling hills.

He was almost to the floor of the valley when off to his right Longarm saw a Circle R rider bearing down on him. The distant bark of his rifle echoed across the grass. With one quick twist, Longarm secured the reins to his saddlehorn, lifted the Winchester from its scabbard, sighted, and fired back at the rider.

But the moonlight played tricks on his eyesight, and he missed.

The rider kept coming and sent another shot at him. Like an angry hornet, the bullet sang past Longarm. Levering another cartridge into the firing chamber, Longarm halted the dun, stood up straight in the stirrups, and squeezed off a shot. This time the rider peeled backward off his mount and vanished into the dark grass.

Two more riders, clearly outlined in the bright moonlight, galloped down on him from the other direction, firing their sixguns rapidly. Slapping his Winchester back into its scabbard, Longarm snatched up his reins and cut away from them, heading for a small gully to his right. He dug his spurs deep and the dun responded magnificently as he lengthened the distance between himself and his two pursuers. Once in the gully, Longarm cut sharply left and flung himself from his horse.

He was crouching behind a boulder when his two pursuers topped the gully's bank, both of them clearly outlined in the moon's silver light. Longarm lifted his Winchester, sighted on the closest rider, and fired. The rider grabbed at his saddlehorn with both hands and plunged forward into the gully.

His companion pulled up abruptly, his horse rearing backward, its forelegs pawing at the air. Somehow the rider managed to wheel his mount and ride back off the rise. As Longarm threw a slug after him, he vanished back into the darkness from which he had come. Longarm moved out from behind the boulder and scrambled up the side of the gully and peered over. The rider was pounding off in a steady gallop, apparently leaving the valley and the Circle R far behind.

Longarm returned to his dun. The horse was trembling, its flanks quivering. The animal had gone a long way that night.

"Just one more run," Longarm whispered to the dun, patting its neck gently. "We'll make it to the house this time."

Mounting up, Longarm charged out of the gully and headed straight for the big house. A single lone rider was charging across the grass toward him. Behind him in the distance, Longarm saw other horsemen riding off, streaming away from the ranch buildings, leaving the Circle R and its troubles behind. Good. That would even matters considerably.

Turning his attention back to the lone rider loping steadily toward him, Longarm realized from his blocky figure and the spray of light hair showing under his hat brim that this was Roebuck's foreman, Tim Prewitt—the one who must have brought those three killers into town.

Longarm spurred his horse to greater speed—directly at the approaching rider. He saw Prewitt's mount waver as the foreman tried to decide in which direction to go in order to avoid a collision. At the last possible moment, Prewitt cut right. Longarm cut left and swept past the foreman, his way to the big house—and J. T. Roebuck—now clear.

He would take care of Roebuck's foreman later.

But Prewitt had a fresh mount. Flinging his horse around, he gave immediate pursuit. By the time Longarm reached the Circle R compound, his dun was laboring. Longarm glanced back. Prewitt was gaining steadily, his sixgun out, gleaming in the bright moonlight. It barked. Longarm ducked forward over the dun's neck, urging it to even greater speed.

Prewitt fired again and this time the bullet plowed into the horse's rump. The dun stumbled once, then went down, throwing Longarm clear. Even as Longarm struck the ground, he was reaching for his Colt. He rolled over once and came up to see Prewitt bearing down on him at full gallop.

He flung up his Colt and fired. The bullet thudded into the horse's chest. The animal appeared to disintegrate under Prewitt, spilling the man almost at Longarm's feet. Longarm stepped closer and kicked Prewitt's Colt out of his grasp. On his feet in an instant, Prewitt charged Longarm like an uncaged wildcat.

Longarm had no time for finesse. He met Prewitt's charge head on and clubbed viciously down with his gun and caught the foreman on the crown of his head. Prewitt rocked back. Longarm stepped closer and struck him again, this time dragging the heavy gunbarrel across Prewitt's face. Prewitt went down on one knee, snarling in sudden pain, then reached out and managed to catch hold of Longarm's gun hand. Longarm yanked it free, stepped back, and fired deliberately down into the man. Prewitt spun about, then struck the ground hard, twisting in pain.

Longarm looked down at the slowly writhing form and thought of Sheriff Bond dying with two slugs in his back and Melissa lying on the floor with a knife-hilt protruding from her breast. He stepped forward deliberately and kicked Prewitt in the face, sending him arching back into the grass, mewling helplessly.

Turning then, he started for the house.

Mounting the verandah steps, he kicked open the front door and stepped into the dark hallway. There was a door to his left. Under the door to his right a sliver of light showed. He pushed the door open.

J. T. Roebuck was sitting at his desk, a huge Colt on the desk in front of him, next to a nearly empty bottle of laudanum. His eyes were wild, bloodshot.

"Hold it right there, Marshal!" he cried.

Longarm pulled up.

"You're trespassin' on my ranch! You don't have a warrant!"

"That's true," Longarm said, calmly closing the door and stepping toward him. "I don't."

"What are you doing here, then?"

Longarm took another step closer and smiled. "I came out here to kill you, Roebuck. But maybe that won't be necessary. Why not come with me? You need help. Admit it. Your reach has exceeded your grasp."

"What the hell are you talking about? You must be mad!"

"There's going to be no railroad, Roebuck," Longarm told him, taking another step closer to the desk. "Don't you see that? Face it, Roebuck. When you had that U.S. marshal killed, you did yourself in as well."

"No!" he cried.

Longarm took another step closer to the man's desk.

Lifting the revolver off the desk, Roebuck fired wildly at Longarm. At that distance he had no business missing, but he did. Longarm reached across the desk and grabbed the man's gun hand, then twisted. With a howl of pain Roebuck dropped his gun and pulled frantically back. In his haste, he fell back over his chair and went down, his shoulder knocking the oil lamp on the shelf beside him to the floor, plunging the room into darkness.

Then the floor blossomed into flames. Shrieking, Roebuck darted out from behind the desk and scrambled through the quaking, livid darkness toward the door and flung it open.

He was greeted by a murderous fusillade.

As the bullets slammed into him, he cried out, then staggered back into the room. Longarm saw a man standing in the hall outside the door, a smoking sixgun in his hand. It was the same oversized sonofabitch Longarm had chased down the hotel's back stairs. The killer stood transfixed, staring in dumb astonishment at the man he had just pumped full of lead.

It appeared he had not expected Roebuck to be the first one to emerge from the room.

Before he could turn his weapon on Longarm, Longarm emptied his .44 into the big fellow's chest. The man crumpled in the doorway, his sixgun clattering to the floor. Ignoring the growing thunder of the fire behind him, Longarm examined Roebuck. He was dead enough. Stepping over the bearlike hulk of the gunman who had killed him, Longarm left the room. Glancing back into it, he saw the flames reaching the wall. It would not be long before they caught the window drapes. Longarm pushed open the outside door and stepped out into the cool, clear night.

He moved past Prewitt's sprawled, dead body and lifted his saddle off the dun. Not a single Circle R rider bothered him. They were dead or long gone. A few minutes later, astride a Circle R horse, Longarm rode out of the horse barn and kept on past the flaming house, a garish light playing across the rutted trace in front of him. Roebuck was getting more than he deserved. A Viking funeral. His corpse was being consumed in flames and there was a dog at his feet.

Without a single glance back, Longarm rode on into the night.

Billy Vail shook his head, then lifted his scotch and finished it.

"I must admit, Longarm," he said, "the heat from Washington did die off pretty quick after you telegraphed me that Roebuck was dead. But you almost played it too damn close to the vest this time."

"Would you rather I let the murderer of Milt Grumman get off scot-free?"

"I would not. You know that. It would not be a good precedent, if you get my meaning."

"That's what I thought."

Longarm waved to the bar girl for another round. Billy Vail did not protest. "You buying, Longarm?"

"I'm buying."

"Well, you don't have to overdo it," he said, smiling. "I told you I wasn't going to pay any attention to those fellers in Washington."

"This is my pleasure, Billy. It's that glad I am to see you."

Their drinks arrived.

Sipping his scotch, Marshal Billy Vail leaned back in the booth, cocked his eye at Longarm, and said, "You know, I still find it hard to believe them chronicles could be so damned important to them Mormons. When I gave them back to those three Mormon officials, you never saw three happier gents. They came all the way from Salt Lake City to pick them up. Said they didn't trust Wells Fargo—if you can imagine such a thing."

Longarm nodded. "Them chronicles were a record of each birth in Idaho Territory in all them Mormon communities Brigham Young insisted was part of his state of Deseret. Melissa told me that those records verified not only each birth, but which wife belonging to which husband did the birthing. Owning them records—or burning them—was the only way Roebuck could dispute Mormon land claims and save himself a pile of money when it came to running his railroad through their land."

Billy Vail shook his head. "Seems like Roebuck went to an awful lot of trouble to save himself a few bucks. Getting Bolen to seduce that girl, and all."

"Well, now, Billy, as I can testify, it wasn't all that difficult for Bolen to seduce Melissa. Not that Bolen ever suspected a thing. She was once Roebuck's mistress."

"My God."

"She hated him, though—and was pretty damn glad when Roebuck let Bolen take his place."

"She told you this, did she?"

"Yes."

Vail shook his head. "Women."

"Just finish your drink, Billy."

The marshal tipped up his glass. Glancing past him, Longarm saw Patricia Fields enter the hotel bar. When she caught sight of Longarm, she brightened. He waved to her, excused himself, and hurried over to greet her.

"My, you look nice," he told her.

"Thank you."

"You finished with bankers for a while?"

"For a while."

"How long do you have before your train pulls out?"

"Darling," she replied, "I have all the time in the world. Paris will wait. I have decided to spend at least a week in Denver—this lovely hotel, especially."

He grinned. "Sounds good. Come on over. Billy's waiting."

Since Longarm first introduced Patricia to him the day before, Billy Vail had been waiting eagerly for this moment. He had left his card with Patricia and this second meeting was the result. He was on his feet now, blushing with pleasure as Longarm escorted Patricia toward him.

She had poured herself into a dark green dress purchased a few days before in Denver's most expensive boutique. A white, broad-brimmed hat framed her gleaming curls, and a folded parasol completed the elegant, stylish outfit. Her waist had been narrowed miraculously by some arcane female magic, causing her bosom to swell to wondrous proportions. As she glided across the room to the booth, she caught every male eye in the place.

After the introductions, she sat down across from Billy Vail. Smiling across the table at him, she leaned forward slightly, giving the man a breathtaking glimpse of her cleft. "It's such a delight to meet you at last, Marshal. Custis has told me so much about you."

"Don't listen to a word this blackguard says."

"Well, I must admit, he was remiss. That is, he didn't really tell me how handsome and gallant a man you are."

Billy Vail blushed with pleasure.

Longarm consulted his watch. "Sorry, you two," he said, "but I have an appointment. I'm late already."

"You mustn't let us detain you," Patricia said. "I'm sure the marshal here will know how to entertain this poor country girl."

"Yeah," said Billy Vail eagerly. "You go right ahead, Custis."

Longarm had never felt more like a fifth wheel.

He left them chattering happily, and a moment later, stepping out into the bracing night air in front of the hotel, he realized that when Patricia Fields did leave this mile-high metropolis for Paris, not only he, but a gruff and legendary U.S. marshal would not be at all happy to see her go.

A pair of flashing blue eyes caught Longarm's attention. He swept off his hat and bowed gallantly to a lovely young blonde in black and gold.

"Why, Dan!" she cried. "How long have you been back?"

"Just a few days."

"I missed you!"

"And I missed you, Carol!"

"It's not Carol, silly. It's Marie."

"Am I forgiven?"

"Of course!"

"Why don't we take a stroll?" he suggested. "The night's cool, and there's a fresh breeze off the mountains."

She snaked a hand through his arm and rested her cheek against his shoulder. "Oh, yes," she sighed happily. "Let's do that."

"Then after, maybe we could—"

"Yes, Dan," she said, her voice eager, "maybe we could."

Longarm strolled off with her into the cool, fragrant night. He wasn't Dan, but he sure as hell wasn't going to tell her that.

Watch for

**LONGARM AND THE HANGMAN'S
VENGEANCE**

one hundred and tenth novel in the bold
LONGARM series from Jove

coming in February!

LONGARM

Explore the exciting Old West with one of the men who made it wild!